Sanctuary

Sanctuary

Edith Wharton

Hesperus Classics

Hesperus Classics
Published by Hesperus Press Limited
4 Rickett Street, London SW6 1RU
www.hesperuspress.com

First published in 1903
First published by Hesperus Press Limited, 2006

Designed and typeset by Fraser Muggeridge studio
Printed in Jordan by Jordan National Press

ISBN: 1-84391-143-4
ISBN13: 978-1-84391-143-2

CONTENTS

FOREWORD

In her autobiography *A Backward Glance* (1934), Edith Wharton remarks that 'the first duty' for any member of the New York society of her youth was 'to maintain a strict standard of uprightness in affairs': what counted above all was 'scrupulous probity' in both business and private life. *Sanctuary* is a two-part laboratory experiment in which this much-vaunted probity is put to the test.

Though set quarter of a century apart, and on different continents, the novella's two sections are cut to the same pattern. Each shows the protagonist grappling with a specific moral dilemma; each dramatises the power struggle between a young woman and her prospective mother-in-law. We first meet Kate Orme at a zenith of happiness. She's about to be married, and her fiancé Denis Peyton has recently inherited a fortune from his stepbrother. The world seems to spin on Kate's behalf: Peyton's 'happy literalness' isn't a flaw so much as an inspired complement to Kate's 'visualising habit'. But the palisade of her well-being is quickly breached. She catches Peyton in a moral lapse; she discovers that the man she's promised to marry is capable of dishonesty and cold self-interest. Struck by the 'irremediableness' of her fiancé's crime, Kate wonders if she should go through with the marriage.

We meet her again, many years later. Kate's son Dick, a young architect in Paris, enters a competition at the Beaux Arts. When his friend Paul Darrow – the 'only rival he feared' – falls ill and dies, entrusting his brilliant designs to Dick, Kate once again faces a test of probity. Darrow's bequest seems to her 'a subtle temptation': should Dick pass off Darrow's drawings as his own, and thereby ensure success in the competition? She feels that 'a crisis in her son's life had been reached' – and yet it's Kate, not Dick, who first perceives and fixates on the opportunity for advancement that Darrow's death has presented. This second quandary seems too coercively engineered: you're never quite convinced that life, rather than Edith Wharton, came up with it.

Both moral challenges pitch Kate into ecstasies of self-examination. Peyton's dishonesty may have had tragic consequences for other people, but to Kate these 'were as nothing in the disaster of [her fiancé's] bright irreclaimableness'. She turns it into *her* tragedy, her spiritual crisis: Denis' revelation occasions in her 'that travail of the soul of which the deeper life is born'. Later, in Paris, it's Dick's future that's at stake, yet Dick exists only as an annex to his mother's self-obsession. She herself describes her love for him as 'a kind of extended egotism'. What admirable moral action does Kate's 'travail' precipitate? None at all. She wants the appearance of 'scrupulous probity' without any correspondent sacrifice of ambition or gratification. Like Lily Bart in *The House of Mirth*, she's designed for 'a situation in which the noblest attitude should also be the easiest'.

Sanctuary was published in October 1903, just after Wharton had started work on *The House of Mirth*. The novella is short on the wit that appears later as the natural dolphin-cresting of her intelligence. But *Sanctuary* gives notice of Wharton's interest in the friction of private needs and public expectations; it provides glimpses of a descriptive ingenuity that can register visible and invisible qualities in the same glance (Denis Peyton's mother 'a scented silvery person whose lavender silks and neutral-tinted manner expressed a mind with its blinds drawn down toward all the unpleasantness of life'); it shows how richly a surprising metaphor can illuminate distinctions of character and feeling: Kate observes of her son that 'the closeness of texture that enabled him to throw off her sarcasms preserved him also from the infiltration of her prejudices'; Mr Orme is 'not a man of subtle perceptions, save where his personal comfort was affected: though his egoism was clothed in the finest feelers, he did not suspect a similar surface in others'.

Best of all, *Sanctuary* gives us Clemence Verney. Clear-sighted, pragmatic, and entirely uninterested in 'the artifices of prudery', Dick's alluring companion sees nothing shameful in her desire to get ahead. She is, Paul Darrow observes, a woman who 'likes to be helped first, and to have everything on her plate at once'. While Kate hides her self-interest under the scarves of her moral scruples, Clemence merrily declares her affection for the outward trappings of success – 'the drums and wreaths and acclamations' – and admits that her attachment to Dick is conditional on his professional achievements. When Kate observes that her son is 'almost too ambitious', Clemence responds crisply: '"Can one be?"' Intelligent, candid, admired for her 'imperviousness' and 'self-command', Clemence threatens the old order by sheer force of style: Kate experiences one conversation with her as 'an actual combat, a measuring of wrist and eye'. *Sanctuary*'s pulse quickens whenever she appears.

At her best, Wharton's metaphors have a burnished elegance and clarity: 'Miss Bart had the gift of following an undercurrent of thought while she appeared to be sailing on the surface of conversation.' But *Sanctuary*'s figurative language can be overwrought and confusing: 'Kate found herself caught in the inexorable continuity of life, found herself gazing over a scene of ruin lit up by the punctual recurrence of habit as nature's calm stare lights the morrow of a whirlwind.'

Later, in *A Backward Glance*, Wharton describes her friendship with a judge named Walter Berry, who would read her manuscripts with forensic attention. 'With each book,' Wharton writes, 'he exacted a higher standard in economy of expression, in purity of language, in the avoidance of the hackneyed and the precious.' *Sanctuary* doesn't always meet the Berry standard. The opening paragraphs, with their surfeit of abstract nouns (happiness, beatitude, peace, joy, confusion, harmony) and imprecisions (seemed, a certain, somehow), are some way from the shimmering specificity of *The House of Mirth* or *The Age of Innocence*. Those novels contain some of the most thrilling prose of the twentieth century. *Sanctuary* is a flexing of wings.

– *William Fiennes, 2006*

Sanctuary

Part One

1

It is not often that youth allows itself to feel undividedly happy: the sensation is too much the result of selection and elimination to be within reach of the awakening clutch on life. But Kate Orme, for once, had yielded herself to happiness, letting it permeate every faculty as a spring rain soaks into a germinating meadow. There was nothing to account for this sudden sense of beatitude, but was it not this precisely that made it so irresistible, so overwhelming? There had been, within the last two months – since her engagement to Denis Peyton – no distinct addition to the sum of her happiness, and no possibility, she would have affirmed, of adding perceptibly to a total already incalculable. Inwardly and outwardly the conditions of her life were unchanged, but whereas, before, the air had been full of flitting wings, now they seemed to pause over her and she could trust herself to their shelter.

Many influences had combined to build up the centre of brooding peace in which she found herself. Her nature answered to the finest vibrations, and at first her joy in loving had been too great not to bring with it a certain confusion, a readjusting of the whole scenery of life. She found herself in a new country, wherein he who had led her there was least able to be her guide. There were moments when she felt that the first stranger in the street could have interpreted her happiness for her more easily than Denis. Then, as her eye adapted itself, as the lines flowed into each other, opening deep vistas upon new horizons, she began to enter into possession of her kingdom, to entertain the actual sense of its belonging to her. But she had never before felt that she also belonged to it, and this was the feeling that now came to complete her happiness, to give it the hallowing sense of permanence.

She rose from the writing-table where, list in hand, she had been going over the wedding invitations, and walked toward the drawing-room window. Everything about her seemed to contribute to that rare harmony of feeling that levied a tax on every sense. The large coolness of the room, its fine traditional air of spacious living, its outlook over field and woodland toward the lake lying under the silver bloom of September; the very scent of the late violets in a glass on the writing-table; the rosy-mauve masses of hydrangea in tubs along the terrace; the fall, now and then, of a leaf through the still air – all, somehow, were mingled in the suffusion of well-being that yet made them seem but so much dross upon its current.

The girl's smile prolonged itself at the sight of a figure approaching from the lower slopes above the lake. The path was a short cut from the Peyton place, and she had known that Denis would appear in it at about that hour. Her smile, however, was prolonged not so much by his approach as by her sense of the impossibility of communicating her mood to him. The feeling did not disturb her. She could not imagine sharing her deepest moods with anyone, and the world in which she lived with Denis was too bright and spacious to admit of any sense of constraint. Her smile was in truth a tribute to that clear-eyed directness of his that was so often a refuge from her own complexities.

Denis Peyton was used to being met with a smile. He might have been pardoned for thinking smiles the habitual wear of the human countenance, and his estimate of life and of himself was necessarily tinged by the cordial terms on which they had always met each other. He had in fact found life, from the start, an uncommonly agreeable business, culminating fitly enough in his engagement to the only girl he had ever wished to marry, and the inheritance, from his unhappy stepbrother, of a fortune that agreeably widened his horizon. Such a combination of circumstances might well justify a young man in thinking himself of some account in the universe, and it seemed the final touch of fitness that the mourning that Denis still wore for poor Arthur should lend a new distinction to his somewhat florid good looks.

Kate Orme was not without an amused perception of her future husband's point of view, but she could enter into it with the tolerance that allows for the inconscient element in all our judgments. There was, for instance, no one more sentimentally humane than Denis' mother, the second Mrs Peyton, a scented silvery person whose lavender silks and neutral-tinted manner expressed a mind with its blinds drawn down toward all the unpleasantness of life; yet it was clear that Mrs Peyton saw a 'dispensation' in the fact that her stepson had never married, and that his death had enabled Denis, at the right moment, to step gracefully into affluence. Was it not, after all, a sign of healthy-mindedness to take the gifts of the gods in this religious spirit, discovering fresh evidence of 'design' in what had once seemed the sad fact of Arthur's inaccessibility to correction? Mrs Peyton, beautifully conscious of having done her 'best' for Arthur, would have thought it unchristian to repine at the providential failure of her efforts. Denis' deductions were, of course, a little less direct than his mother's. He had, besides, been fond of Arthur, and his efforts to keep the poor fellow straight had been less didactic and more spontaneous. Their result read itself, if not in any change in Arthur's character, at least in the revised wording of his will, and Denis' moral sense was pleasantly fortified by the discovery that it very substantially paid to be a good fellow.

The sense of general providentialness on which Mrs Peyton reposed had in fact been confirmed by events that reduced

Denis' mourning to a mere tribute of respect – since it would have been a mockery to deplore the disappearance of anyone who had left behind him such an unsavoury wake as poor Arthur. Kate did not quite know what had happened: her father was as firmly convinced as Mrs Peyton that young girls should not be admitted to any open discussion of life. She could only gather, from the silences and evasions amid which she moved, that a woman had turned up – a woman who was of course 'dreadful', and whose dreadfulness appeared to include a sort of shadowy claim upon Arthur. But the claim, whatever it was, had been promptly discredited. The whole question had vanished and the woman with it. The blinds were drawn again on the ugly side of things, and life was resumed on the usual assumption that no such side existed. Kate knew only that a darkness had crossed her sky and left it as unclouded as before.

Was it, perhaps, she now asked herself, the very lifting of the cloud – remote, unthreatening as it had been – that gave such new serenity to her heaven? It was horrible to think that one's deepest security was a mere sense of escape – that happiness was no more than a reprieve. The perversity of such ideas was emphasised by Peyton's approach. He had the gift of restoring things to their normal relations, of carrying one over the chasms of life through the closed tunnel of an incurious cheerfulness. All that was restless and questioning in the girl subsided in his presence, and she was content to take her love as a gift of grace, which began just where the office of reason ended. She was more than ever, today, in this mood of charmed surrender. More than ever he seemed the keynote of the accord between herself and life, the centre of a delightful complicity in every surrounding circumstance. One could not look at him without seeing that there was always a fair wind in his sails.

It was carrying him toward her, as usual, at a quick confident pace, which nevertheless lagged a little, she noticed, as he emerged from the beech-grove and struck across the lawn. He walked as though he were tired. She had meant to wait for him on the terrace, held in check by her usual inclination to linger on the threshold of her pleasures, but now something drew her toward him, and she went quickly down the steps and across the lawn.

'Denis, you look tired. I was afraid something had happened.'

She had slipped her hand through his arm, and as they moved forward she glanced up at him, struck not so much by any new look in his face as by the fact that her approach had made no change in it.

'I am rather tired. – Is your father in?'

'Papa?' She looked up in surprise. 'He went to town yesterday. Don't you remember?'

'Of course – I'd forgotten. You're alone, then?' She dropped his arm and stood before him. He was very pale now, with the furrowed look of extreme physical weariness.

'Denis – are you ill? *Has* anything happened?'

He forced a smile. 'Yes – but you needn't look so frightened.'

She drew a deep breath of reassurance. *He* was safe, after all! And all else, for a moment, seemed to swing below the rim of her world.

'Your mother – ?' she then said, with a fresh start of fear.

'It's not my mother.' They had reached the terrace, and he moved toward the house. 'Let us go indoors. There's such a beastly glare out here.'

He seemed to find relief in the cool obscurity of the drawing room, where, after the brightness of the afternoon light, their faces were almost indistinguishable to each other. She sat down, and he moved a few paces away. Before the writing-table he paused to look at the neatly sorted heaps of wedding-cards.

'They are to be sent out tomorrow?'

'Yes.'

He turned back and stood before her.

'It's about the woman,' he began abruptly – 'the woman who pretended to be Arthur's wife.'

Kate started as at the clutch of an unacknowledged fear.

'She *was* his wife, then?'

Peyton made an impatient movement of negation. 'If she was, why didn't she prove it? She hadn't a shred of evidence. The courts rejected her appeal.'

'Well, then – ?'

'Well, she's dead.' He paused, and the next words came with difficulty. 'She and the child.'

'The child? There was a child?'

'Yes.'

Kate started up and then sank down. These were not things about which young girls were told. The confused sense of horror had been nothing to this first sharp edge of fact.

'And both are dead?'

'Yes.'

'How do you know? My father said she had gone away – gone back to the West – '

'So we thought. But this morning we found her.'

'Found her?'

He motioned toward the window. 'Out there – in the lake.'

'Both?'

'Both.'

She drooped before him shudderingly, her eyes hidden, as though to exclude the vision. 'She had drowned herself?'

'Yes.'

'Oh, poor thing – poor thing!'

They paused awhile, the minutes delving an abyss between them till he threw a few irrelevant words across the silence.

'One of the gardeners found them.'

'Poor thing!'

'It was sufficiently horrible.'

'Horrible – oh!' She had swung round again to her pole. 'Poor Denis! *You* were not there – *you* didn't have to – ?'

'I had to see her.' She felt the instant relief in his voice. He could talk now, could distend his nerves in the warm air of her sympathy. 'I had to identify her.' He rose nervously and began to pace the room. 'It's knocked the wind out of me. I – my God! I couldn't foresee it, could I?' He halted before her with outstretched hands of argument. 'I did all I could – it's not *my* fault, is it?'

'Your fault? Denis!'

'She wouldn't take the money – ' He broke off, checked by her awakened glance.

'The money? What money?' Her face changed, hardening as his relaxed. 'Had you offered her *money* to give up the case?'

He stared a moment, and then dismissed the implication with a laugh.

'No – no; after the case was decided against her. She seemed hard up, and I sent Hinton to her with a cheque.'

'And she refused it?'

'Yes.'

'What did she say?'

'Oh, I don't know – the usual thing. That she'd only wanted to prove she was his wife – on the child's account. That she'd never wanted his money. Hinton said she was very quiet – not in the least excited – but she sent back the cheque.'

Kate sat motionless, her head bent, her hands clasped about her knees. She no longer looked at Peyton.

'Could there have been a mistake?' she asked slowly.

'A mistake?'

She raised her head now, and fixed her eyes on his, with a strange insistence of observation. 'Could they have been married?'

'The courts didn't think so.'

'Could the courts have been mistaken?'

He started up again, and threw himself into another chair. 'Good God, Kate! We gave her every chance to prove her case – why didn't she do it? You don't know what you're talking about – such things are kept from girls. Why, whenever a man of Arthur's kind dies, such – such women turn up. There are lawyers who live on such jobs – ask your father about it. Of course, this woman expected to be bought off – '

'But if she wouldn't take your money?'

'She expected a big sum, I mean, to drop the case. When she found we meant to fight it, she saw the game was up. I suppose it was her last throw, and she was desperate; we don't know how many times she may have been through the same thing before. That kind of woman is always trying to make money out of the heirs of any man who – who has been about with them.'

Kate received this in silence. She had a sense of walking along a narrow ledge of consciousness above a sheer hallucinating depth into which she dared not look. But the depth drew her, and she plunged one terrified glance into it.

'But the child – the child was Arthur's?'

Peyton shrugged his shoulders. 'There again – how can we tell? Why, I don't suppose the woman herself – I wish to heaven your father were here to explain!'

She rose and crossed over to him, laying her hands on his shoulders with a gesture almost maternal.

'Don't let us talk of it,' she said. 'You did all you could. Think what a comfort you were to poor Arthur.'

He let her hands lie where she had placed them, without response or resistance.

'I tried – I tried hard to keep him straight!'

'We all know that – everyone knows it. And we know how grateful he was – what a difference it made to him in the end. It would have been dreadful to think of his dying out there alone.'

She drew him down on a sofa and seated herself by his side. A deep lassitude was upon him, and the hand she had possessed herself of lay in her hold inert.

'It was splendid of you to travel day and night as you did. And then that dreadful week before he died! But for you he would have died alone among strangers.'

He sat silent, his head dropping forward, his eyes fixed. 'Among strangers,' he repeated absently.

She looked up, as if struck by a sudden thought. 'That poor woman – did you ever see her while you were out there?'

He drew his hand away and gathered his brows together as if in an effort of remembrance.

'I saw her – oh, yes, I saw her.' He pushed the tumbled hair from his forehead and stood up. 'Let us go out,' he said. 'My head is in a fog. I want to get away from it all.'

A wave of compunction drew her to her feet.

'It was my fault! I ought not to have asked so many questions.' She turned and rang the bell. 'I'll order the ponies – we shall have time for a drive before sunset.'

2

With the sunset in their faces they swept through the keen-scented autumn air at the swiftest pace of Kate's ponies. She had given the reins to Peyton, and he had turned the horses' heads away from the lake, rising by woody upland lanes to the high pastures that still held the sunlight. The horses were fresh enough to claim his undivided attention, and he drove in silence, his smooth fair profile turned to his companion, who sat silent also.

Kate Orme was engaged in one of those rapid mental excursions that were forever sweeping her from the straight path of the actual into uncharted regions of conjecture. Her survey of life had always been marked by the tendency to seek out ultimate relations, to extend her researches to the limit of her imaginative experience. But hitherto she had been like some young captive brought up in a windowless palace whose painted walls she takes for the actual world. Now the palace had been shaken to its base, and through a cleft in the walls she looked out upon life. For the first moment all was indistinguishable blackness; then she began to detect vague shapes and confused gestures in the depths. There were people below there, men like Denis, girls like herself – for under the unlikeness she felt the strange affinity – all struggling in that awful coil of moral darkness, with agonised hands reaching up for rescue. Her heart shrank from the horror of it, and then, in a passion of pity, drew back to the edge of the abyss. Suddenly her eyes turned toward Denis. His face was grave, but less disturbed. And men knew about these things! They carried this abyss in their bosoms, and went about smiling, and sat at the feet of innocence. Could it be that Denis – Denis even – Ah, no! She remembered what he had been to poor Arthur; she understood, now, the vague allusions to what he had tried to do for his brother. He had seen Arthur down there, in that coiling blackness, and had leaned over and tried to drag him out. But Arthur was too deep down, and his arms were interlocked with other arms – they had dragged each other deeper, poor souls, like drowning people who fight together in the waves! Kate's visualising habit gave a hateful precision and persistency to the image she had evoked – she could not rid herself of the vision of anguished shapes striving together in the darkness. The horror of it took her by the throat – she drew a choking breath, and felt the tears on her face.

Peyton turned to her. The horses were climbing a hill, and his attention had strayed from them.

'This has done me good,' he began, but as he looked his voice changed. 'Kate! What is it? Why are you crying? Oh, for God's sake, *don't*!' he ended, his hand closing on her wrist.

She steadied herself and raised her eyes to his.

'I – I couldn't help it,' she stammered, struggling in the sudden release of her pent compassion. 'It seems so awful that we should stand so close to this horror – that it might have been you who – '

'I who – what on earth do you mean?' he broke in stridently.

'Oh, don't you see? I found myself exulting that you and I were so far from it – above it – safe in ourselves and each other – and then the other feeling came – the sense of selfishness, of going by on the other side; and I tried to realise that it might have been you and I who – who were down there in the night and the flood – '

Peyton let the whip fall on the ponies' flanks. 'Upon my soul,' he said with a laugh, 'you must have a nice opinion of both of us.'

The words fell chillingly on the blaze of her self-immolation. Would she never learn to remember that Denis was incapable of mounting such hypothetical pyres? He might be as alive as herself to the direct demands of duty, but of its imaginative claims he was robustly unconscious. The thought brought a wholesome reaction of thankfulness.

'Ah, well,' she said, the sunset dilating through her tears, 'don't you see that I can bear to think such things only because they're impossibilities? It's easy to look over into the depths if one has a rampart to lean on. What I most pity poor Arthur for is that, instead of that woman lying there, so dreadfully dead, there might have been a girl like me, so exquisitely alive because of him; but it seems cruel, doesn't it, to let what he was not add ever so little to the value of what you are? To let him contribute ever so little to my happiness by the difference there is between you?'

She was conscious, as she spoke, of straying again beyond his reach, through intricacies of sensation new even to her exploring susceptibilities. A happy literalness usually enabled him to strike a short cut through such labyrinths, and rejoin her smiling on the other side; but now she became wonderingly aware that he had been caught in the thick of her hypothesis.

'It's the difference that makes you care for me, then?' he broke out, with a kind of violence that seemed to renew his clutch on her wrist.

'The difference?'

He lashed the ponies again, so sharply that a murmur escaped her, and he drew them up, quivering, with an inconsequent 'Steady, boys,' at which their back-laid ears protested.

'It's because I'm moral and respectable, and all that, that you're fond of me,' he went on; 'you're – you're simply in love with my virtues. You couldn't imagine caring if I were down there in the ditch, as you say, with Arthur?'

The question fell on a silence that seemed to deepen suddenly within herself. Every thought hung bated on the sense that something was coming: her whole consciousness became a void to receive it.

'Denis!' she cried.

He turned on her almost savagely. 'I don't want your pity, you know,' he burst out. 'You can keep that for Arthur. I had an idea women loved men for themselves – through everything, I mean. But I wouldn't steal your love – I don't want it on false pretences, you understand. Go and look into other men's lives, that's all I ask of you. I slipped into it – it was just a case of holding my tongue when I ought to have spoken – but I – I – for God's sake, don't sit there staring! I suppose you've seen all along that I knew he was married to the woman.'

3

The housekeeper's reminding her that Mr Orme would be at home the next day for dinner, and did she think he would like the venison with claret sauce or jelly, roused Kate to the first consciousness of her surroundings. Her father would return on the morrow: he would give to the dressing of the venison such minute consideration as, in his opinion, every detail affecting his comfort or convenience quite obviously merited. And if it were not the venison it would be something else; if it were not the housekeeper it would be Mr Orme, charged with the results of a conference with his agent, a committee-meeting at his club, or any of the other incidents that, by happening to himself, became events. Kate found herself caught in the inexorable continuity of life, found herself gazing over a scene of ruin lit up by the punctual recurrence of habit as nature's calm stare lights the morrow of a whirlwind.

Life was going on, then, and dragging her at its wheels. She could neither check its rush nor wrench loose from it and drop out – oh, how blessedly – into darkness and cessation. She must go bounding on, racked, broken, but alive in every fibre. The most she could hope was a few hours' respite, not from her own terrors, but from the pressure of outward claims: the midday halt, during which the victim is unbound while his torturers rest from their efforts. Till her father's return she would have the house to herself, and, the question of the venison dispatched, could give herself to long lonely pacings of the empty rooms, and shuddering subsidences upon her pillow.

Her first impulse, as the mist cleared from her brain, was the habitual one of reaching out for ultimate relations. She wanted to know the worst, and for her, as she saw in a flash, the worst of it was the core of fatality in what had happened. She shrank from her own way of putting it – nor was it even figuratively true that she had ever felt, under faith in Denis, any such doubt as the perception implied. But that was merely because her imagination had never put him to the test. She was fond of exposing herself to hypothetical ordeals, but somehow she had never carried Denis with her on these adventures. What she saw now was that, in a world of strangeness, he remained the object least strange to her. She was not in the tragic case of the girl who suddenly sees her lover unmasked. No mask had dropped from Denis' face: the pink shades had simply been lifted from the lamps, and she saw him for the first time in an unmitigated glare.

Such exposure does not alter the features, but it lays an ugly emphasis on the most charming lines, pushing the smile to a grin, the curve of good nature to the droop of slackness. And it was precisely into the flagging lines of extreme weakness that Denis' graceful contour flowed. In the terrible talk that had followed his avowal, and wherein every word flashed a light on his moral processes, she had been less startled by what he had done than by the way in which his conscience had already become a passive surface for the channelling of consequences. He was like a child who had put a match to the curtains, and stands agape at the blaze. It was horribly naughty to put the match – but beyond that the child's responsibility did not extend. In this business of Arthur's, where all had been wrong from the beginning – where self-defence might well find a plea for its casuistries in the absence of a definite right to be measured by – it had been easy, after the first slip, to drop a little lower with each struggle. The woman – oh, the woman was – well, of the kind who prey on such men. Arthur, out there, at his lowest ebb, had drifted into living with her as a man drifts into drink or opium. He knew what she was – he knew where she had come from. But he had fallen ill, and she had nursed him – nursed him devotedly, of course. That was her chance, and she knew it. Before he was out of the fever she had the noose around him – he came to and found himself married. Such cases were common enough – if the man recovered he bought off the woman and got a divorce. It was all a part of the business – the marriage, the bribe, the divorce. Some of those women made a big income out of it – they were married and divorced once a year. If Arthur had only got well – but, instead, he had a relapse and died. And there was the woman, made his widow by mischance as it were, with her child on her arm – whose child? – and a scoundrelly blackmailing lawyer to work up her case for her. Her claim was clear enough – the right of dower, a third of his estate. But if he had never meant to marry her? If he had been trapped as patently as a rustic fleeced in a gambling-hell? Arthur, in his last hours, had confessed to the marriage, but had also acknowledged its folly. And after his death, when Denis came to look about him and make inquiries, he found that the witnesses, if there had been any, were dispersed and undiscoverable. The whole question hinged on Arthur's statement to his brother. Suppress that statement, and the claim vanished, and with it the scandal, the humiliation, the life-long burden of the woman and child dragging the name of Peyton through heaven knew what depths. He had thought of that first, Denis swore, rather than of the money. The money, of course, had made a difference – he was too honest not to own it – but not till afterward, he declared – would have declared on his honour, but that the word tripped him up, and sent a flush to his forehead.

Thus, in broken phrases, he flung his defence at her: a defence improvised, pieced together as he went along, to mask the crude instinctiveness of his act. For with increasing clearness Kate saw, as she listened, that there had been no real struggle in his mind; that, but for the grim logic of chance, he might never have felt the need of any justification. If the woman, after the manner of such baffled huntresses, had wandered off in search of fresh prey, he might, quite sincerely, have congratulated himself on having saved a decent name and an honest fortune from her talons. It was the price she had paid to establish her claim that for the first time brought him to a startled sense of its justice. His conscience responded only to the concrete pressure of facts.

It was with the anguish of this discovery that Kate Orme locked herself in at the end of their talk. How the talk had ended, how at length she had got him from the room and the house, she recalled but confusedly. The tragedy of the woman's death, and of his own share in it, were as nothing in the disaster of his bright irreclaimableness. Once, when she had cried out, 'You would have married me and said nothing,' and he groaned back, 'But I *have* told you,' she felt like a trainer with a lash above some bewildered animal.

But she persisted savagely. 'You told me because you had to; because your nerves gave way; because you knew it couldn't hurt you to tell.' The perplexed appeal of his gaze had almost checked her. 'You told me because it was a relief, but nothing will really relieve you – nothing will really help you – till you have told someone who – who *will* hurt you.'

'Who will hurt me – ?'

'Till you have told the truth as – as openly as you lied.'

He started up, ghastly with fear. 'I don't understand you.'

'You must confess, then – publicly – openly – you must go to the judge. I don't know how it's done.'

'To the judge? When they're both dead? When everything is at an end? What good could that do?' he groaned.

'Everything is not at an end for you – everything is just beginning. You must clear yourself of this guilt, and there is only one way – to confess it. And you must give back the money.'

This seemed to strike him as conclusive proof of her irrelevance. 'I wish I had never heard of the money! But to whom would you have me give it back? I tell you she was a waif out of the gutter. I don't believe anyone knew her real name – I don't believe she had one.'

'She must have had a mother and father.'

'Am I to devote my life to hunting for them through the slums of California? And how shall I know when I have found them? It's impossible to make you understand. I did wrong – I did horribly wrong – but that is not the way to repair it.'

'What is, then?'

He paused, a little askance at the question. 'To do better – to do my best,' he said, with a sudden flourish of firmness. 'To take warning by this dreadful – '

'Oh, be silent,' she cried out, and hid her face. He looked at her hopelessly.

At last he said: 'I don't know what good it can do to go on talking. I have only one more thing to say. Of course you know that you are free.'

He spoke simply, with a sudden return to his old voice and accent, at which she weakened as under a caress. She lifted her head and gazed at him. 'Am I?' she said musingly.

'Kate!' burst from him, but she raised a silencing hand.

'It seems to me,' she said, 'that I am imprisoned – imprisoned with you in this dreadful thing. First I must help you to get out – then it will be time enough to think of myself.'

His face fell and he stammered: 'I don't understand you.'

'I can't say what I shall do – or how I shall feel – till I know what you are going to do and feel.'

'You must see how I feel – that I'm half dead with it.'

'Yes – but that is only half.'

He turned this over for a perceptible space of time before asking slowly: 'You mean that you'll give me up, if I don't do this crazy thing you propose?'

She paused in turn. 'No,' she said; 'I don't want to bribe you. You must feel the need of it yourself.'

'The need of proclaiming this thing publicly?'

'Yes.'

He sat staring before him. 'Of course you realise what it would mean?' he began at length.

'To you?' she returned.

'I put that aside. To others – to you. I should go to prison.'

'I suppose so,' she said simply.

'You seem to take it very easily – I'm afraid my mother wouldn't.'

'Your mother?' This produced the effect he had expected.

'You hadn't thought of her, I suppose? It would probably kill her.'

'It would have killed her to think that you could do what you have done!'

'It would have made her very unhappy, but there's a difference.'

Yes: there was a difference; a difference that no rhetoric could disguise. The secret sin would have made Mrs Peyton wretched, but it would not have killed her. And she would have taken precisely Denis' view of the elasticity of atonement: she would have accepted private regrets as the genteel equivalent of open expiation. Kate could even imagine her extracting a 'lesson' from the providential fact that her son had not been found out.

'You see it's not so simple,' he broke out, with a tinge of doleful triumph.

'No: it's not simple,' she assented.

'One must think of others,' he continued, gathering faith in his argument as he saw her reduced to acquiescence.

She made no answer, and after a moment he rose to go. So far, in retrospect, she could follow the course of their talk, but when, in the act of parting, argument lapsed into entreaty, and renunciation into the passionate appeal to give him at least one more hearing, her memory lost itself in a tumult of pain, and she recalled only that, when the door closed on him, he took with him her promise to see him once again.

4

She had promised to see him again, but the promise did not imply that she had rejected his offer of freedom. In the first rush of misery she had not fully repossessed herself, had felt herself entangled in his fate by a hundred meshes of association and habit, but after a sleepless night spent with the thought of him – that dreadful bridal of their souls – she woke to a morrow in which he had no part. She had not sought her freedom, nor had he given it, but a chasm had opened at their feet, and they found themselves on different sides.

Now she was able to scan the disaster from the melancholy vantage of her independence. She could even draw a solace from the fact that she had ceased to love Denis. It was inconceivable that an emotion so interwoven with every fibre of consciousness should cease as suddenly as the flow of sap in an uprooted plant, but she had never allowed herself to be tricked by the current phraseology of sentiment, and there were no stock axioms to protect her from the truth.

It was probably because she had ceased to love him that she could look forward with a kind of ghastly composure to seeing him again. She had stipulated, of course, that the wedding should be put off, but she had named no other condition beyond asking for two days to herself – two days during which he was not even to write. She wished to shut herself in with her misery, to accustom herself to it as she had accustomed herself to happiness. But actual seclusion was impossible: the subtle reactions of life almost at once began to break down her defences. She could no more have her wretchedness to herself than any other emotion: all the lives about her were so many unconscious factors in her sensations. She tried to concentrate herself on the thought as to how she could best help poor Denis; for love, in ebbing, had laid bare an unsuspected depth of pity. But she found it more and more difficult to consider his situation in the abstract light of right and wrong. Open expiation still seemed to her the only possible way of healing, but she tried vainly to think of Mrs Peyton as taking such a view. Yet Mrs Peyton ought at least to know what had happened: was it not, in the last resort, she who should pronounce on her son's course? For a moment Kate was fascinated by this evasion of responsibility; she had nearly decided to tell Denis that he must begin by confessing everything to his mother. But almost at once she began to shrink from the consequences. There was nothing she so dreaded for him as that anyone should take a light view of his act: should turn its irremediableness into an excuse. And this, she foresaw, was what Mrs Peyton would do. The first burst of misery over, she would envelop the whole situation in a mist of expediency. Brought to the bar of Kate's judgment, she at once revealed herself incapable of higher action.

Kate's conception of her was still under arraignment when the actual Mrs Peyton fluttered in. It was the afternoon of the second day, as the girl phrased it in the dismal recreation of her universe. She had been thinking so hard of Mrs Peyton that the lady's silvery insubstantial presence seemed hardly more than a projection of the thought, but as Kate collected herself, and regained contact with the outer world, her preoccupation yielded to surprise. It was unusual for Mrs Peyton to pay visits. For years she had remained enthroned in a semi-invalidism that prohibited effort while it did not preclude diversion, and the girl at once divined a special purpose in her coming.

Mrs Peyton's traditions would not have permitted any direct method of attack, and Kate had to sit through the usual prelude of ejaculation and anecdote. Presently, however, the elder lady's voice gathered significance, and laying her hand on Kate's she murmured: 'I have come to talk to you of this sad affair.'

Kate began to tremble. Was it possible that Denis had after all spoken? A rising hope checked her utterance, and she saw in a flash that it still lay with him to regain his hold on her. But Mrs Peyton went on delicately: 'It has been a great shock to my poor boy. To be brought in contact with Arthur's past was in itself inexpressibly painful, but this last dreadful business – that woman's wicked act – '

'Wicked?' Kate exclaimed.

Mrs Peyton's gentle stare reproved her. 'Surely religion teaches us that suicide is a sin? And to murder her child! I ought not to speak to you of such things, my dear. No one has ever mentioned anything so dreadful in my presence: my dear husband used to screen me so carefully from the painful side of life. Where there is so much that is beautiful to dwell upon, we should try to ignore the existence of such horrors. But nowadays everything is in the papers, and Denis told me he thought it better that you should hear the news first from him.'

Kate nodded without speaking.

'He felt how *dreadful* it was to have to tell you. But I tell him he takes a morbid view of the case. Of course one is shocked at the woman's crime – but, if one looks a little deeper, how can one help seeing that it may have been designed as the means of rescuing that poor child from a life of vice and misery? That is the view I want Denis to take: I want him to see how all the difficulties of life disappear when one has learned to look for a divine purpose in human sufferings.'

Mrs Peyton rested a moment on this period, as an experienced climber pauses to be overtaken by a less agile companion, but presently she became aware that Kate was still far below her, and perhaps needed a stronger incentive to the ascent.

'My dear child,' she said adroitly, 'I said just now that I was sorry you had been obliged to hear of this sad affair, but after all it is only you who can avert its consequences.'

Kate drew an eager breath. 'Its consequences?' she faltered.

Mrs Peyton's voice dropped solemnly. 'Denis has told me everything,' she said.

'Everything?'

'That you insist on putting off the marriage. Oh, my dear, I do implore you to reconsider that!'

Kate sank back with the sense of having passed again into a region of leaden shadow. 'Is that all he told you?'

Mrs Peyton gazed at her with arch raillery. 'All? Isn't it everything – to him?'

'Did he give you my reason, I mean?'

'He said you felt that, after this shocking tragedy, there ought, in decency, to be a delay, and I quite understand the feeling. It does seem too unfortunate that the woman should have chosen this particular time! But you will find as you grow older that life is full of such sad contrasts.'

Kate felt herself slowly petrifying under the warm drip of Mrs Peyton's platitudes.

'It seems to me,' the elder lady continued, 'that there is only one point from which we ought to consider the question – and that is, its effect on Denis. But for that we ought to refuse to know anything about it. But it has made my boy so unhappy. The lawsuit was a cruel ordeal to him – the dreadful notoriety, the revelation of poor Arthur's infirmities. Denis is as sensitive as a woman; it is his unusual refinement of feeling that makes him so worthy of being loved by you. But such sensitiveness may be carried to excess. He ought not to let this unhappy incident prey on him: it shows a lack of trust in the divine ordering of things. That is what troubles me: his faith in life has been shaken. And – you must forgive me, dear child – you *will* forgive me, I know – but I can't help blaming you a little – '

Mrs Peyton's accent converted the accusation into a caress, which prolonged itself in a tremulous pressure of Kate's hand.

The girl gazed at her blankly. 'You blame *me* – ?'

'Don't be offended, my child. I only fear that your excessive sympathy with Denis, your own delicacy of feeling, may have led you to encourage his morbid ideas. He tells me you were very much shocked – as you naturally would be – as any girl must be – I would not have you otherwise, dear Kate! It is *beautiful* that you should both feel so; most beautiful; but you know religion teaches us not to yield too much to our grief. Let the dead bury their dead; the living owe themselves to each other. And what had this wretched woman to do with either of you? It is a misfortune for Denis to have been connected in any way with a man of Arthur Peyton's character, but after all, poor Arthur did all he could to atone for the disgrace he brought on us, by making Denis his heir – and I am sure I have no wish to question the decrees of Providence.' Mrs Peyton paused again, and then softly absorbed both of Kate's hands. 'For my part,' she continued, 'I see in it another instance of the beautiful ordering of events. Just after dear Denis' inheritance has removed the last obstacle to your marriage, this sad incident comes to show how desperately he needs you, how cruel it would be to ask him to defer his happiness.'

She broke off, shaken out of her habitual placidity by the abrupt withdrawal of the girl's hands. Kate sat inertly staring, but no answer rose to her lips.

At length Mrs Peyton resumed, gathering her draperies about her with a tentative hint of leave-taking: 'I may go home and tell him that you will not put off the wedding?'

Kate was still silent, and her visitor looked at her with the mild surprise of an advocate unaccustomed to plead in vain.

'If your silence means refusal, my dear, I think you ought to realise the responsibility you assume.' Mrs Peyton's voice had acquired an edge of righteous asperity. 'If Denis has a fault it is that he is too gentle, too yielding, too readily influenced by those he cares for. Your influence is paramount with him now – but if you turn from him just when he needs your help, who can say what the result will be?'

The argument, though impressively delivered, was hardly of a nature to carry conviction to its hearer, but it was perhaps for that very reason that she suddenly and unexpectedly replied to it by sinking back into her seat with a burst of tears. To Mrs Peyton, however, tears were the signal of surrender, and, at Kate's side in an instant she hastened to temper her triumph with magnanimity.

'Don't think I don't feel with you, but we must both forget ourselves for our boy's sake. I told him I should come back with your promise.'

The arm she had slipped about Kate's shoulder fell back with the girl's start. Kate had seen in a flash what capital would be made of her emotion.

'No, no, you misunderstand me. I can make no promise,' she declared.

The older lady sat a moment irresolute; then she restored her arm to the shoulder from which it had been so abruptly displaced.

'My dear child,' she said, in a tone of tender confidence, 'if I have misunderstood you, ought you not to enlighten me?

You asked me just now if Denis had given me your reason for this strange postponement. He gave me one reason, but it seems hardly sufficient to explain your conduct. If there is any other – and I know you well enough to feel sure there is – will you not trust me with it? If my boy has been unhappy enough to displease you, will you not give his mother the chance to plead his cause? Remember, no one should be condemned unheard. As Denis' mother, I have the right to ask for your reason.'

'My reason? My reason?' Kate stammered, panting with the exhaustion of the struggle. Oh, if only Mrs Peyton would release her! 'If you have the right to know it, why doesn't he tell you?' she cried.

Mrs Peyton stood up, quivering. 'I will go home and ask him,' she said. 'I will tell him he had your permission to speak.'

She moved toward the door, with the nervous haste of a person unaccustomed to decisive action. But Kate sprang before her.

'No, no; don't ask him! I implore you not to ask him,' she cried.

Mrs Peyton turned on her with sudden authority of voice and gesture. 'Do I understand you?' she said. 'You admit that you have a reason for putting off your marriage, and yet you forbid me – me, Denis' mother – to ask him what it is? My poor child, I needn't ask, for I know already. If he has offended you, and you refuse him the chance to defend himself, I needn't look farther for your reason: it is simply that you have ceased to love him.'

Kate fell back from the door which she had instinctively barricaded.

'Perhaps that is it,' she murmured, letting Mrs Peyton pass.

* * *

Mr Orme's returning carriage-wheels crossed Mrs Peyton's indignant flight, and an hour later Kate, in the bland candle-light of the dinner-hour, sat listening with practised fortitude to her father's comments on the venison.

She had wondered, as she awaited him in the drawing room, if he would notice any change in her appearance. It seemed to her that the flagellation of her thoughts must have left visible traces. But Mr Orme was not a man of subtle perceptions, save where his personal comfort was affected: though his egoism was clothed in the finest feelers, he did not suspect a similar surface in others. His daughter, as part of himself, came within the normal range of his solicitude, but she was an outlying region, a subject province, and Mr Orme's was a highly centralised polity.

News of the painful incident – he often used Mrs Peyton's vocabulary – had reached him at his club, and to some extent disturbed the assimilation of a carefully ordered breakfast, but since then two days had passed, and it did not take Mr Orme forty-eight hours to resign himself to the misfortunes of others. It was all very nasty, of course, and he wished to heaven it hadn't happened to anyone about to be connected with him, but he viewed it with the transient annoyance of a gentleman who has been splashed by the mud of a fatal runaway.

Mr Orme affected, under such circumstances, a bluff and hearty stoicism as remote as possible from Mrs Peyton's deprecating evasion of facts. It was a bad business; he was sorry Kate should have been mixed up with it; but she would be married soon now, and then she would see that life wasn't exactly a Sunday-school story. Everybody was exposed to such disagreeable accidents: he remembered a case in their own family – oh, a distant cousin whom Kate wouldn't have heard of – a poor fellow who had got entangled with just such a woman, and having (most properly) been sent packing by his father, had justified the latter's course by promptly forging his name – a very nasty affair altogether, but luckily the scandal had been hushed up, the woman bought off, and the prodigal, after a season of probation, safely married to a nice girl with a good income, who was told by the family that the doctors recommended his settling in California.

Luckily the scandal was hushed up: the phrase blazed out against the dark background of Kate's misery. That was doubtless what most people felt – the words represented the consensus of respectable opinion. The best way of repairing a fault was to hide it: to tear up the floor and bury the victim at night. Above all, no coroner and no autopsy!

She began to feel a strange interest in her distant cousin. 'And his wife – did she know what he had done?'

Mr Orme stared. His moral pointed, he had returned to the contemplation of his own affairs.

'His wife? Oh, of course not. The secret has been most admirably kept, but her property was put in trust, so she's quite safe with him.'

Her property! Kate wondered if her faith in her husband had also been put in trust, if her sensibilities had been protected from his possible inroads.

'Do you think it quite fair to have deceived her in that way?'

Mr Orme gave her a puzzled glance: he had no taste for the by-paths of ethical conjecture.

'His people wanted to give the poor fellow another chance; they did the best they could for him.'

'And – he has done nothing dishonourable since?'

'Not that I know of: the last I heard was that they had a little boy, and that he was quite happy. At that distance he's not likely to bother *us*, at all events.'

Long after Mr Orme had left the topic, Kate remained lost in its contemplation. She had begun to perceive that the fair surface of life was honeycombed by a vast system of moral sewage. Every respectable household had its special arrangements for the private disposal of family scandals; it was only among the reckless and improvident that such hygienic precautions were neglected. Who was she to pass judgment on the merits of such a system? The social health must be preserved: the means devised were the result of long experience and the collective instinct of self-preservation. She had meant to tell her father that evening that her marriage had been put off, but she now abstained from doing so, not from any doubt of Mr Orme's acquiescence – he could always be made to feel the force of conventional scruples – but because the whole question sank into insignificance beside the larger issue that his words had raised.

In her own room, that night, she passed through that travail of the soul of which the deeper life is born. Her first sense was of a great moral loneliness – an isolation more complete, more impenetrable, than that in which the discovery of Denis' act had plunged her. For she had vaguely leaned, then, on a collective sense of justice that should respond to her own ideas of right and wrong: she still believed in the logical correspondence of theory and practice. Now she saw that, among those nearest her, there was no one who recognised the moral need of expiation. She saw that to take her father or Mrs Peyton into her confidence would be but to widen the circle of sterile misery in which she and Denis moved. At first the aspect of life thus revealed to her seemed simply mean and base – a world where honour was a pact of silence between adroit accomplices. The network of circumstance had tightened round her, and every effort to escape drew its meshes closer. But as her struggles subsided she felt the spiritual release that comes with acceptance: not connivance in dishonour, but recognition of evil. Out of that dark vision light was to come, the shaft of cloud turning to the pillar of fire. For here, at last, life lay before her as it was: not brave, garlanded and victorious, but naked, grovelling and diseased, dragging its maimed limbs through the mud, yet lifting piteous hands to the stars. Love itself, once throned aloft on an altar of dreams, how it stole to her now, storm-beaten and scarred, pleading for the shelter of her breast! Love, indeed, not in the old sense in which she had conceived it, but a graver, austerer presence – the charity of the mystic three. She thought she had ceased to love Denis – but what had she loved in him but her happiness and his? Their affection had been the *garden enclosed* of the Canticles, where they were to walk forever in a delicate isolation of bliss. But now love appeared to her as something more than this – something wider, deeper, more enduring than the selfish passion of a man and a woman. She saw it in all its far-reaching issues, till the first meeting of two pairs of young eyes kindled a light that might be a high-lifted beacon across dark waters of humanity.

All this did not come to her clearly, consecutively, but in a series of blurred and shifting images. Marriage had meant to her, as it means to girls brought up in ignorance of life, simply the exquisite prolongation of wooing. If she had looked beyond, to the vision of wider ties, it was as a traveller gazes over a land veiled in golden haze, and so far distant that the imagination delays to explore it. But now through the blur of sensations one image strangely persisted – the image of Denis' child. Had she ever before thought of their having a child? She could not remember. She was like one who wakens from a long fever: she recalled nothing of her former self or of her former feelings. She knew only that the vision persisted – the vision of the child whose mother she was not to be. It was impossible that she should marry Denis – her inmost soul rejected him... but it was just because she was not to be the child's mother that its image followed her so pleadingly. For she saw with perfect clearness the inevitable course of events. Denis would marry someone else – he was one of the men who are fated to marry, and she needed not his mother's reminder that her abandonment of him at an emotional crisis would fling him upon the first sympathy within reach. He would marry a girl who knew nothing of his secret – for Kate was intensely aware that he would never again willingly confess himself – he would marry a girl who trusted him and leaned on him, as she, Kate Orme – the earlier Kate Orme – had done but two days since! And with this deception between them their child would be born: born to an inheritance of secret weakness, a vice of the moral fibre, as it might be born with some hidden physical taint that would destroy it before the cause should be detected... Well, and what of it? Was she to hold herself responsible? Were not thousands of children born with some such unsuspected taint?... Ah, but if here was one that she could save? What if she, who had had so exquisite a vision of wifehood, should reconstruct from its ruins this vision of protecting maternity – if her love for her lover should be, not lost, but transformed, enlarged, into this passion of charity for his race? If she might expiate and redeem his fault by becoming a refuge from its consequences? Before this strange extension of her love all the old limitations seemed to fall.

Something had cleft the surface of self, and there welled up the mysterious primal influences, the sacrificial instinct of her sex, a passion of spiritual motherhood that made her long to fling herself between the unborn child and its fate...

She never knew, then or after, how she reached this mystic climax of effacement; she was only conscious, through her anguish, of that lift of the heart that made one of the saints declare that joy was the inmost core of sorrow. For it was indeed a kind of joy she felt, if old names must serve for such new meanings; a surge of liberating faith in life, the old *credo quia absurdum*[1] that is the secret cry of all supreme endeavour.

Part Two

1

'Does it look nice, mother?'

Dick Peyton met her with the question on the threshold, drawing her gaily into the little square room, and adding, with a laugh with a blush in it: 'You know she's an uncommonly noticing person, and little things tell with her.'

He swung round on his heel to follow his mother's smiling inspection of the apartment.

'She seems to have *all* the qualities,' Mrs Denis Peyton remarked, as her circuit finally brought her to the prettily appointed tea-table.

'*All*,' he declared, taking the sting from her emphasis by his prompt adoption of it. Dick had always had a wholesome way of thus appropriating to his own use such small shafts of maternal irony as were now and then aimed at him.

Kate Peyton laughed and loosened her furs. 'It looks charmingly,' she pronounced, ending her survey by an approach to the window, which gave, far below, the oblique perspective of a long side-street leading to Fifth Avenue.

The high-perched room was Dick Peyton's private office, a retreat partitioned off from the larger enclosure in which, under a north light and on a range of deal tables, three or four young draughtsmen were busily engaged in elaborating his architectural projects. The outer door of the office bore the sign: *Peyton and Gill, Architects*; but Gill was a utilitarian person, as unobtrusive as his name, who contented himself with a desk in the work-room, and left Dick to lord it alone in the small apartment to which clients were introduced, and where the social part of the business was carried on.

It was to serve, on this occasion, as the scene of a tea designed, as Kate Peyton was vividly aware, to introduce a certain young lady to the scene of her son's labours. Mrs Peyton had been hearing a great deal lately about Clemence Verney. Dick was naturally expansive, and his close intimacy with his mother – an intimacy fostered by his father's early death – if it had suffered some natural impairment in his school and college days, had of late been revived by four years of comradeship in Paris, where Mrs Peyton, in a tiny apartment of the Rue de Varennes, had kept house for him during his course of studies at the Beaux Arts. There were indeed not lacking critics of her own sex who accused Kate Peyton of having figured too largely in her son's life; of having failed to efface herself at a period when it is agreed that young men are best left free to try conclusions with the world. Mrs Peyton, had she cared to defend herself, might have said that Dick, if communicative, was not impressionable, and that the closeness of texture that enabled him to throw off her sarcasms preserved him also from the infiltration of her prejudices. He was certainly no knight of the apron string, but a seemingly resolute and self-sufficient young man, whose romantic friendship with his mother had merely served to throw a veil of suavity over the hard angles of youth.

But Mrs Peyton's real excuse was after all one that she would never have given. It was because her intimacy with her son was the one need of her life that she had, with infinite tact and discretion, but with equal persistency, clung to every step of his growth, dissembling herself, adapting herself, rejuvenating herself in the passionate effort to be always within reach, but never in the way.

Denis Peyton had died after seven years of marriage, when his boy was barely six. During those seven years he had managed to squander the best part of the fortune he had inherited from his stepbrother, so that, at his death, his widow and son were left with a scant competence. Mrs Peyton, during her husband's life, had apparently made no effort to restrain his expenditure. She had even been accused by those judicious persons who are always ready with an estimate of their neighbours' motives, of having encouraged poor Denis' improvidence for the gratification of her own ambition. She had in fact, in the early days of their marriage, tried to launch him in politics, and had perhaps drawn somewhat heavily on his funds in the first heat of the contest, but the experiment ending in failure, as Denis Peyton's experiments were apt to end, she had made no further demands on his exchequer. Her personal tastes were in fact unusually simple, but her outspoken indifference to money was not, in the opinion of her critics, designed to act as a check upon her husband, and it resulted in leaving her, at his death, in straits from which it was impossible not to deduce a moral.

Her small means, and the care of the boy's education, served the widow as a pretext for secluding herself in a socially remote suburb, where it was inferred that she was expiating, on queer food and in ready-made boots, her rash defiance of fortune. Whether or not Mrs Peyton's penance took this form, she hoarded her substance to such good purpose that she was not only able to give Dick the best of schooling, but to propose, on his leaving Harvard, that he should prolong his studies by another four years at the Beaux Arts. It had been the joy of her life that her boy had early shown a marked bent for a special line of work. She could not have borne to see him reduced to a mere money-getter, yet she was not sorry that their small means forbade the cultivation of an ornamental leisure. In his college days Dick had troubled her by a superabundance of tastes, a restless flitting from one form of artistic expression to another. Whatever art he enjoyed he wished to practise, and he passed from music to painting, from painting to architecture, with an ease that seemed to his mother to indicate lack of purpose rather than excess of talent. She had observed that these changes were usually due, not to self-criticism, but to some external discouragement. Any depreciation of his work was enough to convince him of the uselessness of pursuing that special form of art, and the reaction produced the immediate conviction that he was really destined to shine in some other line of work. He had thus swung from one calling to another till, at the end of his college career, his mother took the decisive step of transplanting him to the Beaux Arts, in the hope that a definite course of study, combined with the stimulus of competition, might fix his wavering aptitudes. The result justified her expectation, and their four years in the Rue de Varennes yielded the happiest confirmation of her belief in him. Dick's ability was recognised not only by his mother, but by his professors. He was engrossed in his work, and his first successes developed his capacity for application. His mother's only fear was that praise was still too necessary to him. She was uncertain how long his ambition would sustain him in the face of failure. He gave lavishly where he was sure of a return, but it remained to be seen if he were capable of production without recognition. She had brought him up in a wholesome scorn of material rewards, and nature seemed, in this direction, to have seconded her training. He was genuinely indifferent to money, and his enjoyment of beauty was of that happy sort which does not generate the wish for possession. As long as the inner eye had food for contemplation, he cared very little for the deficiencies in his surroundings; or, it might rather be said, he felt, in the sum total of beauty about him, an ownership of appreciation that left him free from the fret of personal desire. Mrs Peyton had cultivated to excess this disregard of material conditions, but she now began to ask herself whether, in so doing, she had not laid too great a strain on a temperament naturally exalted. In guarding against other tendencies she had perhaps fostered in him too exclusively those qualities that circumstances had brought to an unusual development in herself. His enthusiasms and his disdains were alike too unqualified for that happy mean of character that is the best defence against the surprises of fortune. If she had taught him to set an exaggerated value on ideal rewards, was not that but a shifting of the danger-point on which her fears had always hung? She trembled sometimes to think how little love and a lifelong vigilance had availed in the deflecting of inherited tendencies.

Her fears were in a measure confirmed by the first two years of their life in New York, and the opening of his career as a professional architect. Close on the easy triumphs of his studentships there came the chilling reaction of public indifference. Dick, on his return from Paris, had formed a partnership with an architect who had had several years of practical training in a New York office, but the quiet and industrious Gill, though he attracted to the new firm a few small jobs that overflowed from the business of his former employer, was not able to infect the public with his own faith in Peyton's talents, and it was trying to a genius who felt himself capable of creating palaces to have to restrict his efforts to the building of suburban cottages or the planning of cheap alterations in private houses.

Mrs Peyton expended all the ingenuities of tenderness in keeping up her son's courage, and she was seconded in the task by a friend whose acquaintance Dick had made at the Beaux Arts, and who, two years before the Peytons, had returned to New York to start on his own career as an architect. Paul Darrow was a young man full of crude seriousness, who, after a youth of struggling work and study in his native northwestern state, had won a scholarship that sent him abroad for a course at the Beaux Arts. His two years there coincided with the first part of Dick's residence, and Darrow's gifts had at once attracted the younger student. Dick was unstinted in his admiration of rival talent, and Mrs Peyton, who was romantically given to the cultivation of such generosities, had seconded his enthusiasm by the kindest offers of hospitality to the young student. Darrow thus became the grateful frequenter of their little *salon*, and after their return to New York the intimacy between the young men was renewed, though Mrs Peyton found it more difficult to coax Dick's friend to her New York drawing room than to the informal surroundings of the Rue de Varennes. There, no doubt, secluded and absorbed in her son's work, she had seemed to Darrow almost a fellow-student, but seen among her own associates she became once more the woman of fashion, divided from him by the whole breadth of her ease and his awkwardness. Mrs Peyton, whose tact had divined the cause of his estrangement, would not for an instant let it affect the friendship of the two young men. She encouraged Dick to frequent Darrow, in whom she divined a persistency of effort, an artistic self-confidence, in curious contrast to his social hesitancies. The example of his obstinate capacity for work was just the influence her son needed, and if Darrow would not come to them she insisted that Dick must seek him out, must never let him think that any social discrepancy could affect a friendship based on deeper things. Dick, who had all the loyalties, and who took an honest pride in his friend's growing success, needed no urging to maintain the intimacy, and his copious reports of midnight colloquies in Darrow's lodgings showed Mrs Peyton that she had a strong ally in her invisible friend.

It had been, therefore, somewhat of a shock to learn in the course of time that Darrow's influence was being shared, if not counteracted, by that of a young lady in whose honour Dick was now giving his first professional tea. Mrs Peyton had heard a great deal about Miss Clemence Verney, first from the usual purveyors of such information, and more recently from her son, who, probably divining that rumour had been before him, adopted his usual method of disarming his mother by taking her into his confidence. But, ample as her information was, it remained perplexing and contradictory, and even her own few meetings with the girl had not helped her to a definite opinion. Miss Verney, in conduct and ideas, was patently of the 'new school': a young woman of feverish activities and broadcast judgments, whose very versatility made her hard to define. Mrs Peyton was shrewd enough to allow for the accidents of environment; what she wished to get at was the residuum of character beneath Miss Verney's shifting surface.

'It looks charmingly,' Mrs Peyton repeated, giving a loosening touch to the chrysanthemums in a tall vase on her son's desk.

Dick laughed, and glanced at his watch.

'They won't be here for another quarter of an hour. I think I'll tell Gill to clean out the work-room before they come.'

'Are we to see the drawings for the competition?' his mother asked.

He shook his head smilingly. 'Can't – I've asked one or two of the Beaux Arts fellows, you know, and besides, old Darrow's actually coming.'

'Impossible!' Mrs Peyton exclaimed.

'He swore he would last night.' Dick laughed again, with a tinge of self-satisfaction. 'I've an idea he wants to see Miss Verney.'

'Ah,' his mother murmured. There was a pause before she added: 'Has Darrow really gone in for this competition?'

'Rather! I should say so! He's simply working himself to the bone.'

Mrs Peyton sat revolving her muff on a meditative hand; at length she said: 'I'm not sure I think it quite nice of him.'

Her son halted before her with an incredulous stare. '*Mother*!' he exclaimed.

The rebuke sent a blush to her forehead. 'Well – considering your friendship – and everything.'

'Everything? What do you mean by everything? The fact that he had more ability than I have and is therefore more likely to succeed? The fact that he needs the money and the success a deuced sight more than any of us? Is that the reason you think he oughtn't to have entered? Mother! I never heard you say an ungenerous thing before.'

The blush deepened to crimson, and she rose with a nervous laugh. 'It *was* ungenerous,' she conceded. 'I suppose I'm jealous for you. I hate these competitions!'

Her son smiled reassuringly. 'You needn't. I'm not afraid: I think I shall pull it off this time. In fact, Paul's the only man I'm afraid of – I'm always afraid of Paul – but the mere fact that he's in the thing is a tremendous stimulus.'

His mother continued to study him with an anxious tenderness. 'Have you worked out the whole scheme? Do you *see* it yet?'

'Oh, broadly, yes. There's a gap here and there – a hazy bit, rather – it's the hardest problem I've ever had to tackle; but then it's my biggest opportunity, and I've simply *got* to pull it off!'

Mrs Peyton sat silent, considering his flushed face and illumined eye, which were rather those of the victor nearing the goal than of the runner just beginning the race. She remembered something that Darrow had once said of him: 'Dick always sees the end too soon.'

'You haven't too much time left,' she murmured.

'Just a week. But I shan't go anywhere after this. I shall renounce the world.' He glanced smilingly at the festal tea-table and the embowered desk. 'When I next appear, it will either be with my heel on Paul's neck – poor old Paul – or else – or else – being dragged lifeless from the arena!'

His mother nervously took up the laugh with which he ended. 'Oh, not lifeless,' she said.

His face clouded. 'Well, maimed for life, then,' he muttered.

Mrs Peyton made no answer. She knew how much hung on the possibility of his winning the competition that for weeks past had engrossed him. It was a design for the new museum of sculpture, for which the city had recently voted half a million. Dick's taste ran naturally to the grandiose, and the erection of public buildings had always been the object of his ambition. Here was an unmatched opportunity, and he knew that, in a competition of the kind, the newest man had as much chance of success as the firm of most established reputation, since every competitor entered on his own merits, the designs being submitted to a jury of architects who voted on them without knowing the names of the contestants. Dick, characteristically, was not afraid of the older firms; indeed, as he had told his mother, Paul Darrow was the only rival he feared. Mrs Peyton knew that, to a certain point, self-confidence was a good sign, but somehow her son's did not strike her as being of the right substance – it seemed to have no dimension but extent. Her fears were complicated by a suspicion that, under his professional eagerness for success, lay the knowledge that Miss Verney's favour hung on the victory. It was that, perhaps, which gave a feverish touch to his ambition, and Mrs Peyton, surveying the future from the height of her material apprehensions, divined that the situation depended mainly on the girl's view of it. She would have given a great deal to know Clemence Verney's conception of success.

2

Miss Verney, when she presently appeared, in the wake of the impersonal and exclamatory young married woman who served as a background to her vivid outline, seemed competent to impart at short notice any information required of her. She had never struck Mrs Peyton as more alert and efficient. A melting grace of line and colour tempered her edges with the charming haze of youth, but it occurred to her critic that she might emerge from this morning mist as a dry and metallic old woman.

If Miss Verney suspected a personal application in Dick's hospitality, it did not call forth in her the usual tokens of self-consciousness. Her manner may have been a shade more vivid than usual, but she preserved all her bright composure of glance and speech, so that one guessed, under the rapid dispersal of words, an undisturbed steadiness of perception. She was lavishly but not indiscriminately interested in the evidences of her host's industry, and as the other guests assembled, straying with vague ejaculations through the labyrinth of scale drawings and blueprints, Mrs Peyton noted that Miss Verney alone knew what these symbols stood for.

To his visitors' requests to be shown his plans for the competition, Peyton had opposed a laughing refusal, enforced by the presence of two fellow-architects, young men with lingering traces of the Beaux Arts in their costume and vocabulary, who stood about in Gavarni[2] attitudes and dazzled the ladies by allusions to fenestration and entasis. The party had already drifted back to the tea-table when a hesitating knock announced Darrow's approach. He entered with his usual air of having blundered in by mistake, embarrassed by his hat and greatcoat, and thrown into deeper confusion by the necessity of being introduced to the ladies grouped about the urn. To the men he threw a gruff nod of fellowship, and Dick having relieved him of his encumbrances, he retreated behind the shelter of Mrs Peyton's welcome. The latter judiciously gave him time to recover, and when she turned to him he was engaged in a surreptitious inspection of Miss Verney, whose dusky slenderness, relieved against the bare walls of the office, made her look like a young St John of Donatello's.[3] The girl returned his look with one of her clear glances, and the group having presently broken up again, Mrs Peyton saw that she had drifted to Darrow's side. The visitors at length wandered back to the work-room to see a portfolio of Dick's water-colours, but Mrs Peyton remained seated behind the urn, listening to the interchange of talk through the open door while she tried to coordinate her impressions.

She saw that Miss Verney was sincerely interested in Dick's work: it was the nature of her interest that remained in doubt. As if to solve this doubt, the girl presently reappeared alone on the threshold, and discovering Mrs Peyton, advanced toward her with a smile.

'Are you tired of hearing us praise Mr Peyton's things?' she asked, dropping into a low chair beside her hostess. 'Unintelligent admiration must be a bore to people who know, and Mr Darrow tells me you are almost as learned as your son.'

Mrs Peyton returned the smile, but evaded the question. 'I should be sorry to think your admiration unintelligent,' she said. 'I like to feel that my boy's work is appreciated by people who understand it.'

'Oh, I have the usual smattering,' said Miss Verney carelessly. 'I *think* I know why I admire his work, but then I am sure I see more in it when someone like Mr Darrow tells me how remarkable it is.'

'Does Mr Darrow say that?' the mother exclaimed, losing sight of her object in the rush of maternal pleasure.

'He has said nothing else: it seems to be the only subject that loosens his tongue. I believe he is more anxious to have your son win the competition than to win it himself.'

'He is a very good friend,' Mrs Peyton assented. She was struck by the way in which the girl led the topic back to the special application of it that interested her. She had none of the artifices of prudery.

'He feels sure that Mr Peyton *will* win,' Miss Verney continued. 'It was very interesting to hear his reasons. He is an extraordinarily interesting man. It must be a tremendous incentive to have such a friend.'

Mrs Peyton hesitated. 'The friendship is delightful, but I don't know that my son needs the incentive. He is almost too ambitious.'

Miss Verney looked up brightly. 'Can one be?' she said. 'Ambition is so splendid! It must be so glorious to be a man and go crashing through obstacles, straight up to the thing one is after. I'm afraid I don't care for people who are superior to success. I like marriage by capture!' She rose with her wandering laugh, and stood flushed and sparkling above Mrs Peyton, who continued to gaze at her gravely.

'What do you call success?' the latter asked. 'It means so many different things.'

'Oh, yes, I know – the inward approval, and all that. Well, I'm afraid I like the other kind: the drums and wreaths and acclamations. If I were Mr Peyton, for instance, I'd much rather win the competition than – than be as disinterested as Mr Darrow.'

Mrs Peyton smiled. 'I hope you won't tell him so,' she said half seriously. 'He is over-stimulated already; and he is so easily influenced by anyone who – whose opinion he values.'

She stopped abruptly, hearing herself, with a strange inward shock, re-echo the words which another man's mother had once spoken to her. Miss Verney did not seem to take the allusion to herself, for she continued to fix on Mrs Peyton a gaze of impartial sympathy.

'But we can't help being interested!' she declared.

'It's very kind of you; but I wish you would all help him to feel that his competition is after all of very little account compared with other things – his health and his peace of mind, for instance. He is looking horribly used up.'

The girl glanced over her shoulder at Dick, who was just re-entering the room at Darrow's side.

'Oh, do you think so?' she said. 'I should have thought it was his friend who was used up.'

Mrs Peyton followed the glance with surprise. She had been too preoccupied to notice Darrow, whose crudely modelled face was always of a dull pallor, to which his slow-moving grey eye lent no relief except in rare moments of expansion. Now the face had the fallen lines of a death mask, in which only the smile he turned on Dick remained alive, and the sight smote her with compunction. Poor Darrow! He did look horribly fagged out: as if he needed care and petting and good food. No one knew exactly how he lived. His rooms, according to Dick's report, were fireless and ill kept, but he stuck to them because his landlady, whom he had fished out of some financial plight, had difficulty in obtaining other lodgers. He belonged to no clubs, and wandered out alone for his meals, mysteriously refusing the hospitality that his friends pressed on him. It was plain that he was very poor, and Dick conjectured that he sent what he earned to an aunt in his native village, but he was so silent about such matters that, outside of his profession, he seemed to have no personal life.

Miss Verney's companion having presently advised her of the lapse of time, there ensued a general leave-taking, at the close of which Dick accompanied the ladies to their carriage. Darrow was meanwhile blundering into his greatcoat, a process that always threw him into a state of perspiring embarrassment, but Mrs Peyton, surprising him in the act, suggested that he should defer it and give her a few moments' talk.

'Let me make you some fresh tea,' she said, as Darrow blushingly shed the garment, 'and when Dick comes back we'll all walk home together. I've not had a chance to say two words to you this winter.'

Darrow sank into a chair at her side and nervously contemplated his boots. 'I've been tremendously hard at work,' he said.

'I know: *too* hard at work, I'm afraid. Dick tells me you have been wearing yourself out over your competition plans.'

'Oh, well, I shall have time to rest now,' he returned. 'I put the last stroke to them this morning.'

Mrs Peyton gave him a quick look. 'You're ahead of Dick, then.'

'In point of time only,' he said smiling.

'That is in itself an advantage,' she answered with a tinge of asperity. In spite of an honest effort for impartiality she could not, at the moment, help regarding Darrow as an obstacle in her son's path.

'I wish the competition were over!' she exclaimed, conscious that her voice had betrayed her. 'I hate to see you both looking so fagged.'

Darrow smiled again, perhaps at her studied inclusion of himself.

'Oh, *Dick*'s all right,' he said. 'He'll pull himself together in no time.'

He spoke with an emphasis that might have struck her, if her sympathies had not again been deflected by the allusion to her son.

'Not if he doesn't win,' she exclaimed.

Darrow took the tea she had poured for him, knocking the spoon to the floor in his eagerness to perform the feat gracefully. In bending to recover the spoon he struck the tea-table with his shoulder, and set the cups dancing. Having regained a measure of composure, he took a swallow of the hot tea and set it down with a gasp, precariously near the edge of the tea-table. Mrs Peyton rescued the cup, and Darrow, apparently forgetting its existence, rose and began to pace the room. It was always hard for him to sit still when he talked.

'You mean he's so tremendously set on it?' he broke out.

Mrs Peyton hesitated. 'You know him almost as well as I do,' she said. 'He's capable of anything where there is a possibility of success, but I'm always afraid of the reaction.'

'Oh, well, Dick's a man,' said Darrow bluntly. 'Besides, he's going to succeed.'

'I wish he didn't feel so sure of it. You mustn't think I'm afraid for him. He's a man, and I want him to take his chances with other men, but I wish he didn't care so much about what people think.'

'People?'

'Miss Verney, then: I suppose you know.'

Darrow paused in front of her. 'Yes: he's talked a good deal about her. You think she wants him to succeed?'

'At any price!'

He drew his brows together. 'What do you call any price?'

'Well – herself, in this case, I believe.'

Darrow bent a puzzled stare on her. 'You mean she attached that amount of importance to this competition?'

'She seems to regard it as symbolical: that's what I gather. And I'm afraid she's given him the same impression.'

Darrow's sunken face was suffused by his rare smile. 'Oh, well, he'll pull it off then!' he said.

Mrs Peyton rose with a distracted sigh. 'I half hope he won't, for such a motive,' she exclaimed.

'The motive won't show in his work,' said Darrow. He added, after a pause probably devoted to the search for the right word: 'He seems to think a great deal of her.'

Mrs Peyton fixed him thoughtfully. 'I wish I knew what *you* think of her.'

'Why, I never saw her before.'

'No; but you talked with her today. You've formed an opinion: I think you came here on purpose.'

He chuckled joyously at her discernment: she had always seemed to him gifted with supernatural insight. 'Well, I did want to see her,' he owned.

'And what do you think?'

He took a few vague steps and then halted before Mrs Peyton. 'I think,' he said, smiling, 'that she likes to be helped first, and to have everything on her plate at once.'

3

At dinner, with a rush of contrition, Mrs Peyton remembered that she had after all not spoken to Darrow about his health. He had distracted her by beginning to talk of Dick, and besides, much as Darrow's opinions interested her, his personality had never fixed her attention. He always seemed to her simply a vehicle for the transmission of ideas.

It was Dick who recalled her to a sense of her omission by asking if she hadn't thought that old Paul looked rather more ragged than usual.

'He did look tired,' Mrs Peyton conceded. 'I meant to tell him to take care of himself.'

Dick laughed at the futility of the measure. 'Old Paul is never tired: he can work twenty-five hours out of the twenty-four. The trouble with him is that he's ill. Something wrong with the machinery, I'm afraid.'

'Oh, I'm sorry. Has he seen a doctor?'

'He wouldn't listen to me when I suggested it the other day, but he's so deuced mysterious that I don't know what he may have done since.' Dick rose, putting down his coffee-cup and half-smoked cigarette. 'I've half a mind to pop in on him tonight and see how he's getting on.'

'But he lives at the other end of the earth, and you're tired yourself.'

'I'm not tired; only a little strung-up,' he returned, smiling. 'And besides, I'm going to meet Gill at the office by and by and put in a night's work. It won't hurt me to take a look at Paul first.'

Mrs Peyton was silent. She knew it was useless to contend with her son about his work, and she tried to fortify herself with the remembrance of her own words to Darrow: Dick was a man and must take his chance with other men.

But Dick, glancing at his watch, uttered an exclamation of annoyance. 'Oh, by Jove, I shan't have time after all. Gill is waiting for me now; we must have dawdled over dinner.' He went to give his mother a caressing tap on the cheek. 'Now don't worry,' he adjured her; and as she smiled back at him he added with a sudden happy blush: 'She doesn't, you know: she's so sure of me.'

Mrs Peyton's smile faded, and laying a detaining hand on his, she said with sudden directness: 'Sure of you, or of your success?'

He hesitated. 'Oh, she regards them as synonymous. She thinks I'm bound to get on.'

'But if you don't?'

He shrugged laughingly, but with a slight contraction of his confident brows. 'Why, I shall have to make way for someone else, I suppose. That's the law of life.'

Mrs Peyton sat upright, gazing at him with a kind of solemnity. 'Is it the law of love?' she asked.

He looked down on her with a smile that trembled a little. 'My dear romantic mother, I don't want her pity, you know!'

* * *

Dick, coming home the next morning shortly before daylight, left the house again after a hurried breakfast, and Mrs Peyton heard nothing of him till nightfall. He had promised to be back for dinner, but a few moments before eight, as she was coming down to the drawing room, the parlourmaid handed her a hastily pencilled note.

'Don't wait for me,' it ran. 'Darrow is ill and I can't leave him. I'll send a line when the doctor has seen him.'

Mrs Peyton, who was a woman of rapid reactions, read the words with a pang. She was ashamed of the jealous thoughts she had harboured of Darrow, and of the selfishness that had made her lose sight of his troubles in the consideration of Dick's welfare. Even Clemence Verney, whom she secretly accused of a want of heart, had been struck by Darrow's ill looks, while she had had eyes only for her son. Poor Darrow! How cold and self-engrossed he must have thought her! In the first rush of penitence her impulse was to drive at once to his lodgings, but the infection of his own shyness restrained her. Dick's note gave no details; the illness was evidently grave, but might not Darrow regard her coming as an intrusion? To repair her negligence of yesterday by a sudden invasion of his privacy might be only a greater failure in tact, and after a moment of deliberation she resolved on sending to ask Dick if he wished her to go to him.

The reply, which came late, was what she had expected. 'No, we have all the help we need. The doctor has sent a good nurse, and is coming again later. It's pneumonia, but of course he doesn't say much yet. Let me have some beef-juice as soon as the cook can make it.'

The beef-juice ordered and dispatched, she was left to a vigil in melancholy contrast to that of the previous evening. Then she had been enclosed in the narrow limits of her maternal interests; now the barriers of self were broken down, and her personal preoccupations swept away on the current of a wider sympathy. As she sat there in the radius of lamplight that, for so many evenings, had held Dick and herself in a charmed circle of tenderness, she saw that her love for her boy had come to be merely a kind of extended egotism. Love had narrowed instead of widening her, had rebuilt between herself and life the very walls that, years and years before, she had laid low with bleeding fingers. It was horrible, how she had come to sacrifice everything to the one passion of ambition for her boy...

At daylight she sent another messenger, one of her own servants, who returned without having seen Dick. Mr Peyton had sent word that there was no change. He would write later; he wanted nothing. The day wore on drearily. Once Kate found herself computing the precious hours lost to Dick's unfinished task. She blushed at her ineradicable selfishness, and tried to turn her mind to poor Darrow. But she could not master her impulses, and now she caught herself indulging the thought that his illness would at least exclude him from the competition. But no – she remembered that he had said his work was finished. Come what might, he stood in the path of her boy's success. She hated herself for the thought, but it would not down.

Evening drew on, but there was no note from Dick. At length, in the shamed reaction from her fears, she rang for a carriage and went upstairs to dress. She could stand aloof no longer: she must go to Darrow, if only to escape from her wicked thoughts of him. As she came down again she heard Dick's key in the door. She hastened her steps, and as she reached the hall he stood before her without speaking.

She looked at him and the question died on her lips. He nodded, and walked slowly past her.

'There was no hope from the first,' he said.

The next day Dick was taken up with the preparations for the funeral. The distant aunt, who appeared to be Darrow's only relation, had been duly notified of his death, but no answer having been received from her, it was left to his friend to fulfil the customary duties. He was again absent for the best part of the day, and when he returned at dusk Mrs Peyton, looking up from the tea-table behind which she awaited him, was startled by the deep-lined misery of his face.

Her own thoughts were too painful for ready expression, and they sat for a while in a mute community of wretchedness.

'Is everything arranged?' she asked at length.

'Yes. Everything.'

'And you have not heard from the aunt?'

He shook his head.

'Can you find no trace of any other relations?'

'None. I went over all his papers. There were very few, and I found no address but the aunt's.' He sat thrown back in his chair, disregarding the cup of tea she had mechanically poured for him. 'I found this, though,' he added, after a pause, drawing a letter from his pocket and holding it out to her.

She took it doubtfully. 'Ought I to read it?'

'Yes.'

She saw then that the envelope, in Darrow's hand, was addressed to her son. Within were a few pencilled words, dated on the first day of his illness, the morrow of the day on which she had last seen him.

'Dear Dick,' she read, 'I want you to use my plans for the museum if you can get any good out of them. Even if I pull out of this I want you to. I shall have other chances, and I have an idea this one means a lot to you.'

Mrs Peyton sat speechless, gazing at the date of the letter, which she had instantly connected with her last talk with Darrow. She saw that he had understood her, and the thought scorched her to the soul.

'Wasn't it glorious of him?' Dick said.

She dropped the letter, and hid her face in her hands.

4

The funeral took place the next morning, and on the return from the cemetery Dick told his mother that he must go and look over things at Darrow's office. He had heard the day before from his friend's aunt, a helpless person to whom telegraphy was difficult and travel inconceivable, and who, in eight pages of unpunctuated eloquence, made over to Dick what she called the melancholy privilege of winding up her nephew's affairs.

Mrs Peyton looked anxiously at her son. 'Is there no one who can do this for you? He must have had a clerk or someone who knows about his work.'

Dick shook his head. 'Not lately. He hasn't had much to do this winter, and these last months he had chucked everything to work alone over his plans.'

The word brought a faint colour to Mrs Peyton's cheek. It was the first allusion that either of them had made to Darrow's bequest.

'Oh, of course you must do all you can,' she murmured, turning alone into the house.

The emotions of the morning had stirred her deeply, and she sat at home during the day, letting her mind dwell, in a kind of retrospective piety, on the thought of poor Darrow's devotion. She had given him too little time while he lived, had acquiesced too easily in his growing habits of seclusion, and she felt it as a proof of insensibility that she had not been more closely drawn to the one person who had loved Dick as she loved him. The evidence of that love, as shown in Darrow's letter, filled her with a vain compunction. The very extravagance of his offer lent it a deeper pathos. It was wonderful that, even in the urgency of affection, a man of his almost morbid rectitude should have overlooked the restrictions of professional honour, should have implied the possibility of his friend's overlooking them. It seemed to make his sacrifice the more complete that it had, unconsciously, taken the form of a subtle temptation.

The last word arrested Mrs Peyton's thoughts. A temptation? To whom? Not, surely, to one capable, as her son was capable, of rising to the height of his friend's devotion. The offer, to Dick, would mean simply, as it meant to her, the last touching expression of an inarticulate fidelity: the utterance of a love that at last had found its formula. Mrs Peyton dismissed as morbid any other view of the case. She was annoyed with herself for supposing that Dick could be ever so remotely affected by the possibility at which poor Darrow's renunciation hinted. The nature of the offer removed it from practical issues to the idealising region of sentiment.

Mrs Peyton had been sitting alone with these thoughts for the greater part of the afternoon, and dusk was falling when Dick entered the drawing room. In the dim light, with his pallor heightened by the sombre effect of his mourning, he came upon her almost startlingly, with a revival of some long-effaced impression that, for a moment, gave her the sense of struggling among shadows. She did not, at first, know what had produced the effect; then she saw that it was his likeness to his father.

'Well – is it over?' she asked, as he threw himself into a chair without speaking.

'Yes: I've looked through everything.' He leaned back, crossing his hands behind his head, and gazing past her with a look of utter lassitude.

She paused a moment, and then said tentatively: 'Tomorrow you will be able to go back to your work.'

'Oh – my work,' he exclaimed, as if to brush aside an ill-timed pleasantry.

'Are you too tired?'

'No.' He rose and began to wander up and down the room. 'I'm not tired. – Give me some tea, will you?' He paused before her while she poured the cup, and then, without taking it, turned away to light a cigarette.

'Surely there is still time?' she suggested, with her eyes on him.

'Time? To finish my plans? Oh, yes – there's time. But they're not worth it.'

'Not worth it?' She started up, and then dropped back into her seat, ashamed of having betrayed her anxiety. 'They are worth as much as they were last week,' she said with an attempt at cheerfulness.

'Not to me,' he returned. 'I hadn't seen Darrow's then.'

There was a long silence. Mrs Peyton sat with her eyes fixed on her clasped hands, and her son paced the room restlessly.

'Are they so wonderful?' she asked at length.

'Yes.'

She paused again, and then said, lifting a tremulous glance to his face: 'That makes his offer all the more beautiful.'

Dick was lighting another cigarette, and his face was turned from her. 'Yes – I suppose so,' he said in a low tone.

'They were quite finished, he told me,' she continued, unconsciously dropping her voice to the pitch of his.

'Yes.'

'Then they will be entered, I suppose?'

'Of course – why not?' he answered almost sharply.

'Shall you have time to attend to all that and to finish yours too?'

'Oh, I suppose so. I've told you it isn't a question of tune. I see now that mine are not worth bothering with.'

She rose and approached him, laying her hands on his shoulders. 'You are tired and unstrung; how can you judge? Why not let me look at both designs tomorrow?'

Under her gaze he flushed abruptly and drew back with a half-impatient gesture.

'Oh, I'm afraid that wouldn't help me; you'd be sure to think mine best,' he said with a laugh.

'But if I could give you good reasons?' she pressed him.

He took her hand, as if ashamed of his impatience. 'Dear mother, if you had any reasons their mere existence would prove that they were bad.'

His mother did not return his smile. 'You won't let me see the two designs then?' she said with a faint tinge of insistence.

'Oh, of course – if you want to – if you only won't talk about it now! Can't you see that I'm pretty nearly dead beat?' he burst out uncontrollably; and as she stood silent, he added with a weary fall in his voice, 'I think I'll go upstairs and see if I can't get a nap before dinner.'

* * *

Though they had separated upon the assurance that she should see the two designs if she wished it, Mrs Peyton knew they would not be shown to her. Dick, indeed, would not again deny her request, but had he not reckoned on the improbability of her renewing it? All night she lay confronted by that question. The situation shaped itself before her with that hallucinating distinctness that belongs to the midnight vision. She knew now why Dick had suddenly reminded her of his father: had she not once before seen the same thought moving behind the same eyes? She was sure it had occurred to Dick to use Darrow's drawings. As she lay awake in the darkness she could hear him, long after midnight, pacing the floor overhead: she held her breath, listening to the recurring beat of his foot, which seemed that of an imprisoned spirit revolving wearily in the cage of the same thought. She felt in every fibre that a crisis in her son's life had been reached, that the act now before him would have a determining effect on his whole future. The circumstances of her past had raised to clairvoyance her natural insight into human motive, had made of her a moral barometer responding to the faintest fluctuations of atmosphere, and years of anxious meditation had familiarised her with the form that her son's temptations were likely to take. The peculiar misery of her situation was that she could not, except indirectly, put this intuition, this foresight, at his service. It was a part of her discernment to be aware that life is the only real counsellor, that wisdom unfiltered through personal experience does not become a part of the moral tissues. Love such as hers had a great office, the office of preparation and direction, but it must know how to hold its hand and keep its counsel, how to attend upon its object as an invisible influence rather than as an active interference.

All this Kate Peyton had told herself again and again, during those hours of anxious calculation in which she had tried to cast Dick's horoscope, but not in her moments of most fantastic foreboding had she figured so cruel a test of her courage. If her prayers for him had taken precise shape, she might have asked that he should be spared the spectacular, the dramatic appeal to his will power: that his temptations should slip by him in a dull disguise. She had secured him against all ordinary forms of baseness; the vulnerable point lay higher, in that region of idealising egotism that is the seat of life in such natures.

Years of solitary foresight gave her mind a singular alertness in dealing with such possibilities. She saw at once that the peril of the situation lay in the minimum of risk it involved. Darrow had employed no assistant in working out his plans for the competition, and his secluded life made it almost certain that he had not shown them to anyone, and that she and Dick alone knew them to have been completed. Moreover, it was a part of Dick's duty to examine the contents of his friend's office, and in doing this nothing would be easier than to possess himself of the drawings and make use of any part of them that might serve his purpose. He had Darrow's authority for doing so, and though the act involved a slight breach of professional probity, might not his friend's wishes be invoked as a secret justification? Mrs Peyton found herself almost hating poor Darrow for having been the unconscious instrument of her son's temptation. But what right had she, after all, to suspect Dick of considering, even for a moment, the act of which she was so ready to accuse him? His unwillingness to let her see the drawings might have been the accidental result of lassitude and discouragement. He was tired and troubled, and she had chosen the wrong moment to make the request. His want of readiness might even be due to the wish to conceal from her how far his friend had surpassed him. She knew his sensitiveness on this point, and reproached herself for not having foreseen it. But her own arguments failed to convince her. Deep beneath her love for her boy and her faith in him there lurked a nameless doubt. She could hardly now, in looking back, define the impulse upon which she had married Denis Peyton: she knew only that the deeps of her nature had been loosened, and that she had been borne forward on their current to the very fate from which her heart recoiled. But if in one sense her marriage remained a problem, there was another in which her motherhood seemed to solve it. She had never lost the sense of having snatched her child from some dim peril that still lurked and hovered, and he became more closely hers with every effort of her vigilant love. For the act of rescue had not been accomplished once and for all in the moment of immolation: it had not been by a sudden stroke of heroism, but by ever-renewed and indefatigable effort, which she had built up for him the miraculous shelter of her love. And now that it stood there, a hallowed refuge against failure, she could not even set a light in the pane, but must let him grope his way to it unaided.

5

Mrs Peyton's midnight musings summed themselves up in the conclusion that the next few hours would end her uncertainty. She felt the day to be decisive. If Dick offered to show her the drawings, her fears would be proved groundless; if he avoided the subject, they were justified.

She dressed early in order not to miss him at breakfast, but as she entered the dining room the parlourmaid told her that Mr Peyton had overslept himself, and had rung to have his breakfast sent upstairs. Was it a pretext to avoid her? She was vexed at her own readiness to see a portent in the simplest incident, but while she blushed at her doubts she let them govern her. She left the dining-room door open, determined not to miss him if he came downstairs while she was at breakfast; then she went back to the drawing room and sat down at her writing-table, trying to busy herself with some accounts while she listened for his step. Here too she had left the door open, but presently even this slight departure from her daily usage seemed a deviation from the passive attitude she had adopted, and she rose and shut the door. She knew that she could still hear his step on the stairs – he had his father's quick swinging gait – but as she sat listening, and vainly trying to write, the closed door seemed to symbolise a refusal to share in his trial, a hardening of herself against his need of her. What if he should come down intending to speak, and should be turned from his purpose? Slighter obstacles have deflected the course of events in those indeterminate moments when the soul floats between two tides. She sprang up quickly, and as her hand touched the latch she heard his step on the stairs.

When he entered the drawing room she had regained the writing-table and could lift a composed face to his. He came in hurriedly, yet with a kind of reluctance beneath his haste: again it was his father's step. She smiled, but looked away from him as he approached her; she seemed to be reliving her own past as one relives things in the distortion of fever.

'Are you off already?' she asked, glancing at the hat in his hand.

'Yes; I'm late as it is. I overslept myself.' He paused and looked vaguely about the room. 'Don't expect me till late – don't wait dinner for me.'

She stirred impulsively. 'Dick, you're overworking – you'll make yourself ill.'

'Nonsense. I'm as fit as ever this morning. Don't be imagining things.'

He dropped his habitual kiss on her forehead, and turned to go. On the threshold he paused, and she felt that something in him sought her and then drew back. 'Goodbye,' he called to her as the door closed on him.

She sat down and tried to survey the situation divested of her midnight fears. He had not referred to her wish to see the drawings: but what did the omission signify? Might he not have forgotten her request? Was she not forcing the most trivial details to fit in with her apprehensions? Unfortunately for her own reassurance, she knew that her familiarity with Dick's processes was based on such minute observation, and that, to such intimacy as theirs, no indications were trivial. She was as certain as if he had spoken, that when he had left the house that morning he was weighing the possibility of using Darrow's drawings, of supplementing his own incomplete design from the fullness of his friend's invention. And with a bitter pang she divined that he was sorry he had shown her Darrow's letter.

It was impossible to remain face to face with such conjectures, and though she had given up all her engagements during the few days since Darrow's death, she now took refuge in the thought of a concert that was to take place at a friend's house that morning. The music room, when she entered, was thronged with acquaintances, and she found transient relief in that dispersal of attention that makes society an anaesthetic for some forms of wretchedness. Contact with the pressure of busy indifferent life often gives remoteness to questions that have clung as close as the flesh to the bone, and if Mrs Peyton did not find such complete release, she at least interposed between herself and her anxiety the obligation to dissemble it. But the relief was only momentary, and when the first bars of the overture turned from her the smiles of recognition among which she had tried to lose herself, she felt a deeper sense of isolation. The music, which at another time would have swept her away on some rich current of emotion, now seemed to island her in her own thoughts, to create an artificial solitude in which she found herself more immitigably face to face with her fears. The silence, the *recueillement*,[4] about her gave resonance to the inner voices, lucidity to the inner vision, till she seemed enclosed in a luminous empty horizon against which every possibility took the sharp edge of accomplished fact. With relentless precision the course of events was unrolled before her: she saw Dick yielding to his opportunity, snatching victory from dishonour, winning love, happiness and success in the act by which he lost himself. It was all so simple, so easy, so inevitable, that she felt the futility of struggling or hoping against it. He would win the competition, would marry Miss Verney, would press on to achievement through the opening that the first success had made for him.

As Mrs Peyton reached this point in her forecast, she found her outward gaze arrested by the face of the young lady who so dominated her inner vision. Miss Verney, a few rows distant, sat intent upon the music, in that attitude of poised motion that was her nearest approach to repose. Her slender brown profile with its breezy hair, her quick eye, and the lips that seemed to listen as well as speak, all betokened to Mrs Peyton a nature through which the obvious energies blew free, a bare open stretch of consciousness without shelter for tenderer growths. She shivered to think of Dick's frail scruples exposed to those rustling airs. And then, suddenly, a new thought struck her. What if she might turn this force to her own use, make it serve, unconsciously to Dick, as the means of his deliverance? Hitherto she had assumed that her son's worst danger lay in the chance of his confiding his difficulty to Clemence Verney, and she had, in her own past, a precedent that made her think such a confidence not unlikely. If he did carry his scruples to the girl, she argued, the latter's imperviousness, her frank inability to understand them, would have the effect of dispelling them like mist, and he was acute enough to know this and profit by it. So she had hitherto reasoned, but now the girl's presence seemed to clarify her perceptions, and she told herself that something in Dick's nature, something that she herself had put there, would resist this short cut to safety, would make him take the more tortuous way to his goal rather than gain it through the privacies of the heart he loved. For she had lifted him thus far above his father, that it would be a disenchantment to him to find that Clemence Verney did not share his scruples. On this much, his mother now exultingly felt, she could count in her passive struggle for supremacy. No, he would never, never tell Clemence Verney – and his one hope, his sure salvation, therefore lay in someone else's telling her.

The excitement of this discovery had nearly, in mid-concert, swept Mrs Peyton from her seat to the girl's side. Fearing to miss the latter in the throng at the entrance, she slipped out during the last number and, lingering in the farther drawing room, let the dispersing audience drift her in Miss Verney's direction. The girl shone sympathetically on her approach, and in a moment they had detached themselves from the crowd and taken refuge in the perfumed emptiness of the conservatory.

The girl, whose sensations were always easily set in motion, had at first a good deal to say of the music, for which she claimed, on her hearer's part, an active show of approval or dissent, but this dismissed, she turned a melting face on Mrs Peyton and said with one of her rapid modulations of tone: 'I was so sorry about poor Mr Darrow.'

Mrs Peyton uttered an assenting sigh. 'It was a great grief to us – a great loss to my son.'

'Yes – I know. I can imagine what you must have felt. And then it was so unlucky that it should have happened just now.'

Mrs Peyton shot a reconnoitring glance at her profile. 'His dying, you mean, on the eve of success?'

Miss Verney turned a frank smile upon her. 'One ought to feel that, of course – but I'm afraid I am very selfish where my friends are concerned, and I was thinking of Mr Peyton's having to give up his work at such a critical moment.' She spoke without a note of deprecation: there was a pagan freshness in her opportunism.

Mrs Peyton was silent, and the girl continued after a pause: 'I suppose now it will be almost impossible for him to finish his drawings in time. It's a pity he hadn't worked out the whole scheme a little sooner. Then the details would have come of themselves.'

Mrs Peyton felt a contempt strangely mingled with exultation. If only the girl would talk in that way to Dick!

'He has hardly had time to think of himself lately,' she said, trying to keep the coldness out of her voice.

'No, of course not,' Miss Verney assented; 'but isn't that all the more reason for his friends to think of him? It was very dear of him to give up everything to nurse Mr Darrow – but, after all, if a man is going to get on in his career there are times when he must think first of himself.'

Mrs Peyton paused, trying to choose her words with deliberation. It was quite clear now that Dick had not spoken, and she felt the responsibility that devolved upon her.

'Getting on in a career – is that always the first thing to be considered?' she asked, letting her eyes rest musingly on the girl's.

The glance did not disconcert Miss Verney, who returned it with one of equal comprehensiveness. 'Yes,' she said quickly, and with a slight blush. 'With a temperament like Mr Peyton's I believe it is. Some people can pick themselves up after any number of bad falls: I am not sure that he could. I think discouragement would weaken instead of strengthening him.'

Both women had forgotten external conditions in the quick reach for each other's meanings. Mrs Peyton flushed, her maternal pride in revolt, but the answer was checked on her lips by the sense of the girl's unexpected insight. Here was someone who knew Dick as well as she did – should she say a partisan or an accomplice? A dim jealousy stirred beneath

Mrs Peyton's other emotions: she was undergoing the agony that the mother feels at the first intrusion on her privilege of judging her child, and her voice had a flutter of resentment.

'You must have a poor opinion of his character,' she said.

Miss Verney did not remove her eyes, but her blush deepened beautifully. 'I have, at any rate,' she said, 'a high one of his talent. I don't suppose many men have an equal amount of moral and intellectual energy.'

'And you would cultivate the one at the expense of the other?'

'In certain cases – and up to a certain point.' She shook out the long fur of her muff, one of those silvery flexible furs that clothe a woman with a delicate sumptuousness. Everything about her, at the moment, seemed rich and cold – everything, as Mrs Peyton quickly noted, but the blush lingering under her dark skin, and so complete was the girl's self-command that the blush seemed to be there only because it had been forgotten.

'I dare say you think me strange,' she continued. 'Most people do, because I speak the truth. It's the easiest way of concealing one's feelings. I can, for instance, talk quite openly about Mr Peyton under shelter of your inference that I shouldn't do so if I were what is called "interested" in him. And as I *am* interested in him, my method has its advantages!' She ended with one of the fluttering laughs that seemed to flit from point to point of her expressive person.

Mrs Peyton leaned toward her. 'I believe you are interested,' she said quietly; 'and since I suppose you allow others the privilege you claim for yourself, I am going to confess that I followed you here in the hope of finding out the nature of your interest.'

Miss Verney shot a glance at her, and drew away in a soft subsidence of undulating furs.

'Is this an embassy?' she asked smiling.

'No: not in any sense.'

The girl leaned back with an air of relief. 'I'm glad; I should have disliked – ' She looked again at Mrs Peyton. 'You want to know what I mean to do?'

'Yes.'

'Then I can only answer that I mean to wait and see what he does.'

'You mean that everything is contingent on his success?'

'*I* am – if I'm everything,' she admitted gaily.

The mother's heart was beating in her throat, and her words seemed to force themselves out through the throbs.

'I – I don't quite see why you attach such importance to this special success.'

'Because he does,' the girl returned instantly. 'Because to him it is the final answer to his self-questioning – the questioning whether he is ever to amount to anything or not. He says if he has anything in him it ought to come out now. All the conditions are favourable – it is the chance he has always prayed for. You see,' she continued, almost confidentially, but without the least loss of composure – 'you see he has told me a great deal about himself and his various experiments – his phases of indecision and disgust. There are lots of tentative talents in the world, and the sooner they are crushed out by circumstances the better. But it seems as though he really had it in him to do something distinguished – as though the uncertainty lay in his character and not in his talent. That is what interests, what attracts me. One can't teach a man to have genius, but if he has it one may show him how to use it. That is what I should be good for, you see – to keep him up to his opportunities.'

Mrs Peyton had listened with an intensity of attention that left her reply unprepared. There was something startling and yet half attractive in the girl's avowal of principles that are oftener lived by than professed.

'And you think,' she began at length, 'that in this case he has fallen below his opportunity?'

'No one can tell, of course; but his discouragement, his *abattement*,[5] is a bad sign. I don't think he has any hope of succeeding.'

The mother again wavered a moment. 'Since you are so frank,' she then said, 'will you let me be equally so, and ask how lately you have seen him?'

The girl smiled at the circumlocution. 'Yesterday afternoon,' she said simply.

'And you thought him – '

'Horribly down on his luck. He said himself that his brain was empty.'

Again Mrs Peyton felt the throb in her throat, and a slow blush rose to her cheek. 'Was that all he said?'

'About himself – was there anything else?' said the girl quickly.

'He didn't tell you of – of an opportunity to make up for the time he has lost?'

'An opportunity? I don't understand.'

'He didn't speak to you, then, of Mr Darrow's letter?'

'He said nothing of any letter.'

'There *was* one, which was found after poor Darrow's death. In it he gave Dick leave to use his design for the competition. Dick says the design is wonderful – it would give him just what he needs.'

Miss Verney sat listening raptly, with a rush of colour that suffused her like light.

'But when was this? Where was the letter found? He never said a word of it!' she exclaimed.

'The letter was found on the day of Darrow's death.'

'But I don't understand! Why has he never told me? Why should he seem so hopeless?' She turned an ignorant appealing face on Mrs Peyton. It was prodigious, but it was true – she felt nothing, saw nothing, but the crude fact of the opportunity.

Mrs Peyton's voice trembled with the completeness of her triumph. 'I suppose his reason for not speaking is that he has scruples.'

'Scruples?'

'He feels that to use the design would be dishonest.'

Miss Verney's eyes fixed themselves on her in a commiserating stare. 'Dishonest? When the poor man wished it himself? When it was his last request? When the letter is there to prove it? Why, the design belongs to your son! No one else had any right to it.'

'But Dick's right does not extend to passing it off as his own – at least that is his feeling, I believe. If he won the competition he would be winning it on false pretences.'

'Why should you call them false pretences? His design might have been better than Darrow's if he had had time to carry it out. It seems to me that Mr Darrow must have felt this – must have felt that he owed his friend some compensation for the time he took from him. I can imagine nothing more natural than his wishing to make this return for your son's sacrifice.'

She positively glowed with the force of her conviction, and Mrs Peyton, for a strange instant, felt her own resistance wavering. She herself had never considered the question in that light – the light of Darrow's viewing his gift as a justifiable compensation. But the glimpse she caught of it drove her shuddering behind her retrenchments.

'That argument,' she said coldly, 'would naturally be more convincing to Darrow than to my son.'

Miss Verney glanced up, struck by the change in Mrs Peyton's voice.

'Ah, then you agree with him? You think it *would* be dishonest?'

Mrs Peyton saw that she had slipped into self-betrayal. 'My son and I have not spoken of the matter,' she said evasively. She caught the flash of relief in Miss Verney's face.

'You haven't spoken? Then how do you know how he feels about it?'

'I only judge from – well, perhaps from his not speaking.'

The girl drew a deep breath. 'I see,' she murmured. 'That is the very reason that prevents his speaking.'

'The reason?'

'Your knowing what he thinks – and his knowing that you know.'

Mrs Peyton was startled at her subtlety. 'I assure you,' she said, rising, 'that I have done nothing to influence him.'

The girl gazed at her musingly. 'No,' she said with a faint smile, 'nothing except to read his thoughts.'

6

Mrs Peyton reached home in the state of exhaustion that follows on a physical struggle. It seemed to her as though her talk with Clemence Verney had been an actual combat, a measuring of wrist and eye. For a moment she was frightened at what she had done – she felt as though she had betrayed her son to the enemy. But before long she regained her moral balance, and saw that she had merely shifted the conflict to the ground on which it could best be fought out – since the prize fought for was the natural battlefield. The reaction brought with it a sense of helplessness, a realisation that she had let the issue pass out of her hold, but since, in the last analysis, it had never lain there, since it was above all needful that the determining touch should be given by any hand but hers, she presently found courage to subside into inaction. She had done all she could – even more, perhaps, than prudence warranted – and now she could but await passively the working of the forces she had set in motion.

For two days after her talk with Miss Verney she saw little of Dick. He went early to his office and came back late. He seemed less tired, more self-possessed, than during the first days after Darrow's death, but there was a new inscrutableness in his manner, a note of reserve, of resistance almost, as though he had barricaded himself against her conjectures. She had been struck by Miss Verney's reply to the anxious asseveration that she had done nothing to influence Dick – 'Nothing,' the girl had answered, 'except to read his thoughts.' Mrs Peyton shrank from this detection of a tacit interference with her son's liberty of action. She longed – how passionately he would never know – to stand apart from him in this struggle between his two destinies, and it was almost a relief that he on his side should hold aloof, should, for the first time in their relation, seem to feel her tenderness as an intrusion.

Only four days remained before the date fixed for the sending in of the designs, and still Dick had not referred to his work. Of Darrow, also, he had made no mention. His mother longed to know if he had spoken to Clemence Verney – or rather if the girl had forced his confidence. Mrs Peyton was almost certain that Miss Verney would not remain silent – there were times when Dick's renewed application to his work seemed an earnest of her having spoken, and spoken convincingly. At the thought Kate's heart grew chill. What if her experiment should succeed in a sense she had not intended? If the girl should reconcile Dick to his weakness, should pluck the sting from his temptation? In this round of uncertainties the mother revolved for two interminable days, but the second evening brought an answer to her question.

Dick, returning earlier than usual from the office, had found, on the hall table, a note that, since morning, had been under his mother's observation. The envelope, fashionable in tint and texture, was addressed in a rapid staccato hand that seemed the very imprint of Miss Verney's utterance. Mrs Peyton did not know the girl's writing, but such notes had of late lain often enough on the hall table to make their attribution easy. This communication Dick, as his mother poured his tea, looked over with a face of shifting lights; then he folded it into his notecase, and said, with a glance at his watch: 'If you haven't asked anyone for this evening I think I'll dine out.'

'Do, dear; the change will be good for you,' his mother assented.

He made no answer, but sat leaning back, his hands clasped behind his head, his eyes fixed on the fire. Every line of his body expressed a profound physical lassitude, but the face remained alert and guarded. Mrs Peyton, in silence, was busying herself with the details of the tea-making, when suddenly, inexplicably, a question forced itself to her lips.

'And your work – ?' she said, strangely hearing herself speak.

'My work – ?' He sat up, on the defensive almost, but without a tremor of the guarded face.

'You're getting on well? You've made up for lost time?'

'Oh, yes: things are going better.' He rose, with another glance at his watch. 'Time to dress,' he said, nodding to her as he turned to the door.

It was an hour later, during her own solitary dinner, that a ring at the door was followed by the parlourmaid's announcement that Mr Gill was there from the office. In the hall, in fact, Kate found her son's partner, who explained apologetically that he had understood Peyton was dining at home, and had come to consult him about a difficulty that had arisen since he had left the office. On hearing that Dick was out, and that his mother did not know where he had gone, Mr Gill's perplexity became so manifest that Mrs Peyton, after a moment, said hesitatingly: 'He may be at a friend's house; I could give you the address.'

The architect caught up his hat. 'Thank you; I'll have a try for him.'

Mrs Peyton hesitated again. 'Perhaps,' she suggested, 'it would be better to telephone.'

She led the way into the little study behind the drawing room, where a telephone stood on the writing-table. The folding doors between the two rooms were open: should she close them as she passed back into the drawing room? On the threshold she wavered an instant; then she walked on and took her usual seat by the fire.

Gill, meanwhile, at the telephone, had 'rung up' the Verney house, and inquired if his partner were dining there. The reply was evidently affirmative, and a moment later Kate knew that he was in communication with her son. She sat motionless, her hands clasped on the arms of her chair, her head erect, in an attitude of avowed attention. If she listened she would listen openly: there should be no suspicion of eavesdropping. Gill, engrossed in his message, was probably hardly conscious of her presence, but if he turned his head he should at least have no difficulty in seeing her, and in being aware that she could hear what he said. Gill, however, as she was quick to remember, was doubtless ignorant of any need for secrecy in his communication to Dick. He had often heard the affairs of the office discussed openly before Mrs Peyton, had been led to regard her as familiar with all the details of her son's work. He talked on unconcernedly, and she listened.

Ten minutes later, when he rose to go, she knew all that she had wanted to find out. Long familiarity with the technicalities of her son's profession made it easy for her to translate the stenographic jargon of the office. She could lengthen out all Gill's abbreviations, interpret all his allusions, and reconstruct Dick's answers from the questions addressed to him. And when the door closed on the architect she was left face to face with the fact that her son, unknown to anyone but herself, was using Darrow's drawings to complete his work.

* * *

Mrs Peyton, left alone, found it easier to continue her vigil by the drawing-room fire than to carry up to the darkness and silence of her own room the truth she had been at such pains to acquire. She had no thought of sitting up for Dick. Doubtless, his dinner over, he would rejoin Gill at the office, and prolong through the night the task in which she now knew him to be engaged. But it was less lonely by the fire than in the wide-eyed darkness that awaited her upstairs. A mortal loneliness enveloped her. She felt as though she had fallen by the way, spent and broken in a struggle of which even its object had been unconscious. She had tried to deflect the natural course of events, she had sacrificed her personal happiness to a fantastic ideal of duty, and it was her punishment to be left alone with her failure, outside the normal current of human strivings and regrets.

She had no wish to see her son just then: she would have preferred to let the inner tumult subside, to repossess herself in this new adjustment to life, before meeting his eyes again. But as she sat there, far adrift on her misery, she was aroused by the turning of his key in the latch. She started up, her heart sounding a retreat, but her faculties too dispersed to obey it, and while she stood wavering, the door opened and he was in the room.

In the room, and with face illumined: a Dick she had not seen since the strain of the contest had cast its shade on him. Now he shone as in a sunrise of victory, holding out exultant hands from which she hung back instinctively.

'Mother! I knew you'd be waiting for me!' He had her on his breast now, and his kisses were in her hair. 'I've always said you knew everything that was happening to me, and now you've guessed that I wanted you tonight.'

She was struggling faintly against the dear endearments. 'What *has* happened?' she murmured, drawing back for a dazzled look at him.

He had drawn her to the sofa, had dropped beside her, regaining his hold of her in the boyish need that his happiness should be touched and handled.

'My engagement has happened!' he cried out to her. 'You stupid dear, do you need to be told?'

7

She had indeed needed to be told: the surprise was complete and overwhelming. She sat silent under it, her hands trembling in his, till the blood mounted to his face and she felt his confident grasp relax.

'You didn't guess it, then?' he exclaimed, starting up and moving away from her.

'No; I didn't guess it,' she confessed in a dead-level voice.

He stood above her, half challenging, half defensive. 'And you haven't a word to say to me? Mother!' he adjured her.

She rose too, putting her arms about him with a kiss. 'Dick! Dear Dick!' she murmured.

'She imagines you don't like her; she says she's always felt it. And yet she owns you've been delightful, that you've tried to make friends with her. And I thought you knew how much it would mean to me, just now, to have this uncertainty over, and that you'd actually been trying to help me, to put in a good word for me. I thought it was you who had made her decide.'

'I?'

'By your talk with her the other day. She told me of your talk with her.'

His mother's hands slipped from his shoulders and she sank back into her seat. She felt the cruelty of her silence, but only an inarticulate murmur found a way to her lips. Before speaking she must clear a space in the suffocating rush of her sensations. For the moment she could only repeat inwardly that Clemence Verney had yielded before the final test, and that she herself was somehow responsible for this fresh entanglement of fate. For she saw in a flash how the coils of circumstance had tightened, and as her mind cleared it was filled with the perception that this, precisely, was what the girl intended, that this was why she had conferred the crown before the victory. By pledging herself to Dick she had secured his pledge in return: had put him on his honour in a cynical inversion of the term. Kate saw the succession of events spread out before her like a map, and the astuteness of the girl's policy frightened her. Miss Verney had conducted the campaign like a strategist. She had frankly owned that her interest in Dick's future depended on his capacity for success, and in order to key him up to his first achievement she had given him a foretaste of its results.

So much was almost immediately clear to Mrs Peyton, but in a moment her inferences had carried her a point further. For it was now plain to her that Miss Verney had not risked so much without first trying to gain her point at less cost: that if she had had to give herself as a prize, it was because no other bribe had been sufficient. This then, as the mother saw with a throb of hope, meant that Dick, who since Darrow's death had held to his purpose unwaveringly, had been deflected from it by the first hint of Clemence Verney's connivance. Kate had not miscalculated: things had happened as she had foreseen. In the light of the girl's approval his act had taken an odious look. He had recoiled from it, and it was to revive his flagging courage that she had had to promise herself, to take him in the meshes of her surrender.

Kate, looking up, saw above her the young perplexity of her boy's face, the suspended happiness waiting to brim over. With a fresh touch of misery she said to herself that this was his hour, his one irrecoverable moment, and that she was darkening it by her silence. Her memory went back to the same hour in her own life: she could feel its heat in her pulses still. What right had she to stand in Dick's light? Who was she to decide between his code and hers? She put out her hand and drew him down to her.

'She'll be the making of me, you know, mother,' he said, as they leaned together. 'She'll put new life in me – she'll help me get my second wind. Her talk is like a fresh breeze blowing away the fog in my head. I never knew anyone who saw so straight to the heart of things, who had such a grip on values. She goes straight up to life and catches hold of it, and you simply can't make her let go.'

He got up and walked the length of the room; then he came back and stood smiling above his mother.

'You know you and I are rather complicated people,' he said. 'We're always walking around things to get new views of them – we're always rearranging the furniture. And somehow she simplifies life so tremendously.' He dropped down beside her with a deprecating laugh. 'Not that I mean, dear, that it hasn't been good for me to argue things out with myself, as you've taught me to – only the man who stops to talk is apt to get shoved aside nowadays, and I don't believe Milton's archangels would have had much success in active business.'

He had begun in a strain of easy confidence, but as he went on she detected an effort to hold the note, she felt that his words were being poured out in a vain attempt to fill the silence that was deepening between them. She longed, in her turn, to pour something into that menacing void, to bridge it with a reconciling word or look; but her soul hung back, and she had to take refuge in a vague murmur of tenderness.

'My boy! My boy!' she repeated, and he sat beside her without speaking, their hand-clasp alone spanning the distance that had widened between their thoughts.

* * *

The engagement, as Kate subsequently learned, was not to be made known till later. Miss Verney had even stipulated that for the present there should be no recognition of it in her own family or in Dick's. She did not wish to interfere with his final work for the competition, and had made him promise, as he laughingly owned, that he would not see her again till the drawings were sent in. His mother noticed that he made no other allusion to his work, but when he bade her goodnight he added that he might not see her the next morning, as he had to go to the office early. She took this as a hint that he wished to be left alone, and kept her room the next day till the closing door told her that he was out of the house.

She herself had waked early, and it seemed to her that the day was already old when she came downstairs. Never had the house appeared so empty. Even in Dick's longest absences something of his presence had always hung about the rooms: a fine dust of memories and associations, which wanted only the evocation of her thought to float into a palpable semblance of him. But now he seemed to have taken himself quite away, to have broken every fibre by which their lives had hung together. Where the sense of him had been there was only a deeper emptiness: she felt as if a strange man had gone out of her house.

She wandered from room to room, aimlessly, trying to adjust herself to their solitude. She had known such loneliness before, in the years when most women's hearts are fullest; but that was long ago, and the solitude had after all been less complete, because of the sense that it might still be filled. Her son had come: her life had brimmed over; but now the tide ebbed again, and she was left gazing over a bare stretch of wasted years. Wasted! There was the mortal pang, the stroke from which there was no healing. Her faith and hope had been marsh lights luring her to the wilderness, her love a vain edifice reared on shifting ground.

In her round of the rooms she came at last to Dick's study upstairs. It was full of his boyhood: she could trace the history of his past in its quaint relics and survivals, in the school books lingering on his crowded shelves, the school photographs and college trophies hung among his later treasures. All his successes and failures, his exaltations and inconsistencies, were recorded in the warm huddled heterogeneous room. Everywhere she saw the touch of her own hand, the vestiges of her own steps. It was she alone who held the clue to the labyrinth, who could thread a way through the confusions and contradictions of his past, and her soul rejected the thought that his future could ever escape from her. She dropped down into his shabby college armchair and hid her face in the papers on his desk.

8

The day dwelt in her memory as a long stretch of aimless hours: blind alleys of time that led up to a dead wall of inaction.

Toward afternoon she remembered that she had promised to dine out and go to the opera. At first she felt that the contact of life would be unendurable; then she shrank from shutting herself up with her misery. In the end she let herself drift passively on the current of events, going through the mechanical routine of the day without much consciousness of what was happening.

At twilight, as she sat in the drawing room, the evening paper was brought in, and in glancing over it her eye fell on a paragraph that seemed printed in more vivid type than the rest. It was headed *The New Museum of Sculpture*, and underneath she read:

> The artists and architects selected to pass on the competitive designs for the new Museum will begin their sittings on Monday, and tomorrow is the last day on which designs may

be sent in to the committee. Great interest is felt in the competition, as the conspicuous site chosen for the new building, and the exceptionally large sum voted by the city for its erection, offer an unusual field for the display of architectural ability.

She leaned back, closing her eyes. It was as though a clock had struck, loud and inexorably, marking off some irrecoverable hour. She was seized by a sudden longing to seek Dick out, to fall on her knees and plead with him: it was one of those physical obsessions against which the body has to stiffen its muscles as well as the mind its thoughts. Once she even sprang up to ring for a cab, but she sank back again, breathing as if after a struggle, and gripping the arms of her chair to keep herself down.

'I can only wait for him – only wait for him – ' she heard herself say, and the words loosened the sobs in her throat.

At length she went upstairs to dress for dinner. A ghostlike self looked back at her from her toilet glass: she watched it performing the mechanical gestures of the toilet, dressing her, as it appeared, without help from her actual self. Each little act stood out sharply against the blurred background of her brain: when she spoke to her maid her voice sounded extraordinarily loud. Never had the house been so silent; or, stay – yes, once she had felt the same silence, once when Dick, in his school days, had been ill of a fever, and she had sat up with him on the decisive night. The silence had been as deep and as terrible then, and as she dressed she had before her the vision of his room, of the cot in which he lay, of his restless head working a hole in the pillow, his face so pinched and alien under the familiar freckles. It might be his death watch she was keeping: the doctors had warned her to be ready. And in the silence her soul had fought for her boy, her love had hung over him like wings, her abundant useless hateful life had struggled to force itself into his empty veins. And she had succeeded, she had saved him, she had poured her life into him; and in place of the strange child she had watched all night, at daylight she held her own boy to her breast.

That night had once seemed to her the most dreadful of her life, but she knew now that it was one of the agonies that enrich, that the passion thus spent grows fourfold from its ashes. She could not have borne to keep this new vigil alone. She must escape from its sterile misery, must take refuge in other lives till she regained courage to face her own. At the opera, in the illumination of the first entr'acte, as she gazed about the house, wondering through the numb ache of her wretchedness how others could talk and smile and be indifferent, it seemed to her that all the jarring animation about her was suddenly focused in the face of Clemence Verney. Miss Verney sat opposite, in the front of a crowded box, a box in which, continually, the black-coated background shifted and renewed itself. Mrs Peyton felt a throb of anger at the girl's bright air of unconcern. She forgot that she too was talking, smiling, holding out her hand to newcomers, in a studied mimicry of life, while her real self played out its tragedy behind the scenes. Then it occurred to her that, to Clemence Verney, there was no tragedy in the situation. According to the girl's calculations, Dick was virtually certain of success, and unsuccess was to her the only conceivable disaster.

All through the opera the sense of that opposing force, that negation of her own beliefs, burned itself into Mrs Peyton's consciousness. The space between herself and the girl seemed to vanish, the throng about them to disperse, till they were face to face and alone, enclosed in their mortal enmity. At length the feeling of humiliation and defeat grew unbearable to Mrs Peyton. The girl seemed to flout her in the insolence of victory, to sit there as the visible symbol of her failure. It was better after all to be at home alone with her thoughts.

As she drove away from the opera she thought of that other vigil that, only a few streets away, Dick was perhaps still keeping. She wondered if his work were over, if the final stroke had been drawn. And as she pictured him there, signing his pact with evil in the loneliness of the conniving night, an uncontrollable impulse possessed her. She must drive by his windows and see if they were still alight. She would not go up to him – she dared not – but at least she would pass near to him, would invisibly share his watch and hover on the edge of his thoughts. She lowered the window and called out the address to the coachman.

The tall office building loomed silent and dark as she approached it; but presently, high up, she caught a light in the familiar windows. Her heart gave a leap, and the light swam on her through tears. The carriage drew up, and for a moment she sat motionless. Then the coachman bent down toward her, and she saw that he was asking if he should drive on. She tried to shape a yes, but her lips refused it, and she shook her head. He continued to lean down perplexedly, and at length, under the interrogation of his attitude, it became impossible to sit still, and she opened the door and stepped out. It was equally impossible to stand on the sidewalk, and her next steps carried her to the door of the building. She groped for the bell and rang it, feeling still dimly accountable to the coachman for some consecutiveness of action, and after a moment the nightwatchman opened the door, drawing back amazed at the shining apparition that confronted him. Recognising Mrs Peyton, whom he had seen about the building by day, he tried to adapt himself to the situation by a vague stammer of apology.

'I came to see if my son is still here,' she faltered.

'Yes, ma'am, he's here. He's been here most nights lately till after twelve.'

'And is Mr Gill with him?'

'No: Mr Gill he went away just after I come on this evening.'

She glanced up into the cavernous darkness of the stairs.

'Is he alone up there, do you think?'

'Yes, ma'am, I know he's alone, because I seen his men leaving soon after Mr Gill.'

Kate lifted her head quickly. 'Then I will go up to him,' she said.

The watchman apparently did not think it proper to offer any comment on this unusual proceeding, and a moment later she was fluttering and rustling up through the darkness, like a nightbird hovering among rafters. There were ten flights to climb: at every one her breath failed her, and she had to stand still and press her hands against her heart. Then the weight on her breast lifted, and she went on again, upward and upward, the great dark building dropping away from her, in tier after tier of mute doors and mysterious corridors. At last she reached Dick's floor, and saw the light shining down the passage from his door. She leaned against the wall, her breath coming short, the silence throbbing in her ears. Even now it was not too late to turn back. She bent over the stairs, letting her eyes plunge into the nether blackness, with the single glimmer of the watchman's lights in its depths; then she turned and stole toward her son's door.

There again she paused and listened, trying to catch, through the hum of her pulses, any noise that might come to her from within. But the silence was unbroken – it seemed as though the office must be empty. She pressed her ear to the door, straining for a sound. She knew he never sat long at his work, and it seemed unaccountable that she should not hear him moving about the drawing board. For a moment she fancied he might be sleeping, but sleep did not come to him readily after prolonged mental effort – she recalled the restless straying of his feet above her head for hours after he returned from his night work in the office.

She began to fear that he might be ill. A nervous trembling seized her, and she laid her hand on the latch, whispering 'Dick!'

Her whisper sounded loudly through the silence, but there was no answer, and after a pause she called again. With each call the hush seemed to deepen: it closed in on her, mysterious and impenetrable. Her heart was beating in short frightened leaps: a moment more and she would have cried out. She drew a quick breath and turned the door-handle.

The outer room, Dick's private office, with its red carpet and easy chairs, stood in pleasant lamplit emptiness. The last time she had entered it, Darrow and Clemence Verney had been there, and she had sat behind the urn observing them. She paused a moment, struck now by a fault sound from beyond; then she slipped noiselessly across the carpet, pushed open the swinging door, and stood on the threshold of the work-room. Here the gaslights hung a green-shaded circle of brightness over the great draughting table in the middle of the floor. Table and floor were strewn with a confusion of papers – torn blueprints and tracings, crumpled sheets of tracing paper wrenched from the draughting boards in a sudden fury of destruction; and in the centre of the havoc, his arms stretched across the table and his face hidden in them, sat Dick Peyton.

He did not seem to hear his mother's approach, and she stood looking at him, her breast tightening with a new fear.

'Dick!' she said, 'Dick! – ' and he sprang up, staring with dazed eyes. But gradually, as his gaze cleared, a light spread in it, a mounting brightness of recognition.

'You've come – you've come – ' he said, stretching his hands to her, and all at once she had him in her breast as in a shelter.

'You wanted me?' she whispered as she held him.

He looked up at her, tired, breathless, with the white radiance of the runner near the goal.

'I *had* you, dear!' he said, smiling strangely on her, and her heart gave a great leap of understanding.

Her arms had slipped from his neck, and she stood leaning on him, deep-suffused in the shyness of her discovery. For it might still be that he did not wish her to know what she had done for him.

But he put his arm about her, boyishly, and drew her toward one of the hard seats between the tables; and there, on the bare floor, he knelt before her, and hid his face in her lap. She sat motionless, feeling the dear warmth of his head against her knees, letting her hands stray in faint caresses through his hair.

Neither spoke for awhile; then he raised his head and looked at her. 'I suppose you know what has been happening to me,' he said.

She shrank from seeming to press into his life a hair's breadth further than he was prepared to have her go. Her eyes turned from him toward the scattered drawings on the table.

'You have given up the competition?' she said.

'Yes – and a lot more.' He stood up, the wave of emotion ebbing, yet leaving him nearer, in his recovered calmness, than in the shock of their first moment.

'I didn't know, at first, how much you guessed,' he went on quietly. 'I was sorry I'd shown you Darrow's letter, but it didn't worry me much because I didn't suppose you'd think it possible that I should – take advantage of it. It's only lately that I've understood that you knew everything.' He looked at her with a smile. 'I don't know yet how I found it out, for you're wonderful about keeping things to yourself, and you never made a sign. I simply felt it in a kind of nearness – as if I couldn't get away from you. Oh, there were times when I should have preferred not having you about – when I tried to turn my back on you, to see things from other people's standpoint. But you were always there – you wouldn't be discouraged. And I got tired of trying to explain things to you, of trying to bring you round to my way of thinking. You wouldn't go away and you wouldn't come any nearer – you just stood there and watched everything that I was doing.'

He broke off, taking one of his restless turns down the long room. Then he drew up a chair beside her, and dropped into it with a great sigh.

'At first, you know, I hated it most awfully. I wanted to be let alone and to work out my own theory of things. If you'd said a word – if you'd tried to influence me – the spell would have been broken. But just because the actual *you* kept apart and didn't meddle or pry, the other, the you in my heart, seemed to get a tighter hold on me. I don't know how to tell you – it's all mixed up in my head – but old things you'd said and done kept coming back to me, crowding between me and what I was trying for, looking at me without speaking, like old friends I'd gone back on, till I simply couldn't stand it any longer. I fought it off till tonight, but when I came back to finish the work there you were again – and suddenly, I don't know how, you weren't an obstacle any longer, but a refuge – and I crawled into your arms as I used to when things went against me at school.'

His hands stole back into hers, and he leaned his head against her shoulder like a boy.

'I'm an abysmally weak fool, you know,' he ended; 'I'm not worth the fight you've put up for me. But I want you to know that it's your doing – that if you had let go an instant I should have gone under – and that if I'd gone under I should never have come up again alive.'

NOTES

1. I believe it because it is absurd (Latin).
2. Pseudonym of Sulpice Guillaume Chevalier (1804–66), French caricaturist and lithographer.
3. Italian sculptor (*c.*1386–1466).
4. Contemplation, reverence (French).
5. Despondency (French).

BIOGRAPHICAL NOTE

Edith Wharton (née Newbold Jones) was born in 1862 into a wealthy New York family. She was educated privately in New York and Europe, and in 1885 she married Edward Robbins Wharton, a banker from Boston. They settled in France in 1907 but the marriage was a troubled one, and they eventually divorced in 1913, due partly to Edward's mental ill heath, and partly to Edith's struggles to balance the duties of a wife with her ambitions as a writer. She had published her first book, *The Decoration of Houses*, in 1897.

After her divorce, Edith continued to live in France, where she would remain until her death. She took on the role of literary hostess and her Paris home saw frequent visits from Henry James, Walter Berry and a number of other writers. She herself had gained a considerable reputation as a writer with a number of books behind her: *The Greater Inclination* had appeared in 1899, followed by *The Touchstone* (1900), and, in 1905, *The House of Mirth*. France provided the setting for a number of her novels, *Madame de Treymes* (1907) and *The Reef* (1912) among them.

During the First World War she worked for various American newspapers, and became involved in work with refugees. She continued to write novels and in 1920 produced perhaps her most famous novel, *The Age of Innocence*, which went on to win the Pulitzer Prize. This study of New York society life brilliantly encapsulated many of her themes and concerns as a writer. These, and in particular the role of women in turn-of-the-century America, she also explored in her numerous short stories.

She was still working on her final novel, *The Buccaneers*, when she died on 11th August 1937.

SELECTED TITLES FROM HESPERUS PRESS

Author	*Title*	*Foreword writer*
Pedro Antonio de Alarcón	*The Three-Cornered Hat*	
Louisa May Alcott	*Behind a Mask*	Doris Lessing
Dante Alighieri	*New Life*	Louis de Bernières
Dante Alighieri	*The Divine Comedy: Inferno*	Ian Thomson
Edmondo de Amicis	*Constantinople*	Umberto Eco
Gabriele D'Annunzio	*The Book of the Virgins*	Tim Parks
Pietro Aretino	*The School of Whoredom*	Paul Bailey
Pietro Aretino	*The Secret Life of Nuns*	
Pietro Aretino	*The Secret Life of Wives*	Paul Bailey
Jane Austen	*Lady Susan*	
Jane Austen	*Lesley Castle*	Zoë Heller
Jane Austen	*Love and Friendship*	Fay Weldon
Honoré de Balzac	*Colonel Chabert*	A.N. Wilson
Charles Baudelaire	*On Wine and Hashish*	Margaret Drabble
Aphra Behn	*The Lover's Watch*	
Giovanni Boccaccio	*Life of Dante*	A.N. Wilson
Charlotte Brontë	*The Foundling*	
Charlotte Brontë	*The Green Dwarf*	Libby Purves
Charlotte Brontë	*The Secret*	Salley Vickers
Charlotte Brontë	*The Spell*	Nicola Barker
Emily Brontë	*Poems of Solitude*	Helen Dunmore
Giacomo Casanova	*The Duel*	Tim Parks
Miguel de Cervantes	*The Dialogue of the Dogs*	Ben Okri
Geoffrey Chaucer	*The Parliament of Birds*	
Anton Chekhov	*The Story of a Nobody*	Louis de Bernières
Anton Chekhov	*Three Years*	William Fiennes
Wilkie Collins	*The Frozen Deep*	
Wilkie Collins	*A Rogue's Life*	Peter Ackroyd

Wilkie Collins	*Who Killed Zebedee?*	Martin Jarvis
William Congreve	*Incognita*	Peter Ackroyd
Joseph Conrad	*Heart of Darkness*	A.N. Wilson
Joseph Conrad	*The Return*	Colm Tóibín
James Fenimore Cooper	*Autobiography of a Pocket Handkerchief*	Ruth Scurr
Daniel Defoe	*The King of Pirates*	Peter Ackroyd
Charles Dickens	*The Haunted House*	Peter Ackroyd
Charles Dickens	*A House to Let*	
Charles Dickens	*Mrs Lirriper*	Philip Hensher
Charles Dickens	*Mugby Junction*	Robert Macfarlane
Charles Dickens	*The Wreck of the Golden Mary*	Simon Callow
Emily Dickinson	*The Single Hound*	Andrew Motion
Fyodor Dostoevsky	*The Double*	Jeremy Dyson
Fyodor Dostoevsky	*The Gambler*	Jonathan Franzen
Fyodor Dostoevsky	*Notes from the Underground*	Will Self
Fyodor Dostoevsky	*Poor People*	Charlotte Hobson
Arthur Conan Doyle	*The Mystery of Cloomber*	
Arthur Conan Doyle	*The Tragedy of the Korosko*	Tony Robinson
Alexandre Dumas	*Captain Pamphile*	Tony Robinson
Alexandre Dumas	*One Thousand and One Ghosts*	
Joseph von Eichendorff	*Life of a Good-for-nothing*	
George Eliot	*Amos Barton*	Matthew Sweet
George Eliot	*Mr Gilfil's Love Story*	Kirsty Gunn
J. Meade Falkner	*The Lost Stradivarius*	Tom Paulin
Henry Fielding	*Jonathan Wild the Great*	Peter Ackroyd
Gustave Flaubert	*Memoirs of a Madman*	Germaine Greer
Gustave Flaubert	*November*	Nadine Gordimer
E.M. Forster	*Arctic Summer*	Anita Desai

Ugo Foscolo	*Last Letters of Jacopo Ortis*	Valerio Massimo Manfredi
Giuseppe Garibaldi	*My Life*	Tim Parks
Elizabeth Gaskell	*Lois the Witch*	Jenny Uglow
Theophile Gautier	*The Jinx*	Gilbert Adair
André Gide	*Theseus*	
Johann Wolfgang von Goethe	*The Man of Fifty*	A.S. Byatt
Nikolai Gogol	*The Squabble*	Patrick McCabe
Thomas Hardy	*Fellow-Townsmen*	Emma Tennant
L.P. Hartley	*Simonetta Perkins*	Margaret Drabble
Nathaniel Hawthorne	*Rappaccini's Daughter*	Simon Schama
E.T.A. Hoffmann	*Mademoiselle de Scudéri*	Gilbert Adair
Victor Hugo	*The Last Day of a Condemned Man*	Libby Purves
Joris-Karl Huysmans	*With the Flow*	Simon Callow
Henry James	*In the Cage*	Libby Purves
John Keats	*Fugitive Poems*	Andrew Motion
D.H. Lawrence	*Daughters of the Vicar*	Anita Desai
D.H. Lawrence	*The Fox*	Doris Lessing
Giacomo Leopardi	*Thoughts*	Edoardo Albinati
Mikhail Lermontov	*A Hero of Our Time*	Doris Lessing
Nikolai Leskov	*Lady Macbeth of Mtsensk*	Gilbert Adair
Jack London	*Before Adam*	
Niccolò Machiavelli	*Life of Castruccio Castracani*	Richard Overy
Xavier de Maistre	*A Journey Around my Room*	Alain de Botton
Edgar Lee Masters	*Spoon River Anthology*	Shena Mackay
Guy de Maupassant	*Butterball*	Germaine Greer
Lorenzino de' Medici	*Apology for a Murder*	Tim Parks
Herman Melville	*The Enchanted Isles*	Margaret Drabble
Prosper Mérimée	*Carmen*	Philip Pullman

Sir Thomas More	*The History of Richard III*	Sister Wendy Beckett
Sándor Petofi	*John the Valiant*	George Szirtes
Francis Petrarch	*My Secret Book*	Germaine Greer
Edgar Allan Poe	*Eureka*	Sir Patrick Moore
Alexander Pope	*Scriblerus*	Peter Ackroyd
Alexander Pope	*The Rape of the Lock and A Key to the Lock*	Peter Ackroyd
Antoine François Prévost	*Manon Lescaut*	Germaine Greer
Marcel Proust	*Pleasures and Days*	A.N. Wilson
Alexander Pushkin	*Dubrovsky*	Patrick Neate
Alexander Pushkin	*Ruslan and Lyudmila*	Colm Tóibín
François Rabelais	*Gargantua*	Paul Bailey
François Rabelais	*Pantagruel*	Paul Bailey
Christina Rossetti	*Commonplace*	Andrew Motion
Marquis de Sade	*Betrayal*	John Burnside
Marquis de Sade	*Incest*	Janet Street-Porter
George Sand	*The Devil's Pool*	Victoria Glendinning
Saki	*A Shot in the Dark*	Jeremy Dyson
Friedrich von Schiller	*The Ghost-seer*	Martin Jarvis
Mary Shelley	*Transformation*	
Percy Bysshe Shelley	*Zastrozzi*	Germaine Greer
Stendhal	*Memoirs of an Egotist*	Doris Lessing
Robert Louis Stevenson	*Dr Jekyll and Mr Hyde*	Helen Dunmore
Theodor Storm	*The Lake of the Bees*	Alan Sillitoe
Italo Svevo	*A Perfect Hoax*	Tim Parks
Jonathan Swift	*Directions to Servants*	Colm Tóibín
W.M. Thackeray	*Rebecca and Rowena*	Matthew Sweet
Leo Tolstoy	*The Death of Ivan Ilyich*	Nadine Gordimer
Leo Tolstoy	*The Forged Coupon*	Andrew Miller
Leo Tolstoy	*Hadji Murat*	Colm Tóibín
Ivan Turgenev	*Faust*	Simon Callow

Mark Twain	*The Diary of Adam and Eve*	John Updike
Mark Twain	*Tom Sawyer, Detective*	
Jules Verne	*A Fantasy of Dr Ox*	Gilbert Adair
Leonardo da Vinci	*Prophecies*	Eraldo Affinati
Edith Wharton	*The Touchstone*	Salley Vickers
Oscar Wilde	*The Portrait of Mr W.H.*	Peter Ackroyd
Virginia Woolf	*Carlyle's House and Other Sketches*	Doris Lessing
Virginia Woolf	*Monday or Tuesday*	Scarlett Thomas
Virginia Woolf, Vanessa Bell with Thoby Stephen	*Hyde Park Gate News*	Hermione Lee
Emile Zola	*The Dream*	Tim Parks
Emile Zola	*For a Night of Love*	A.N. Wilson